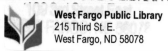

W9-BSN-371

Praise for Ed McBain & the 87th Precinct

"Raw and realistic...The bad guys are very bad, and the good guys are better." —*Detroit Free Press*

"Ed McBain's 87th Precinct series...simply the best police procedurals being written in the United States." —*Washington Post*

"The best crime writer in the business." —*Houston Post*

"Ed McBain is a national treasure." —*Mystery News*

"It's hard to think of anyone better at what he does. In fact, it's impossible."—Robert B. Parker

"I never read Ed McBain without the awful thought that I still have a lot to learn. And when you think you're catching up, he gets better."
—Tony Hillerman

"McBain is the unquestioned king...light years ahead of anyone else in the field." —*San Diego Union-Tribune*

"McBain tells great stories." —Elmore Leonard

"Pure prose poetry...It is such writers as McBain who bring the great American urban mythology to life." —*The London Times*

"The McBain stamp: sharp dialogue and crisp plotting."
—*Miami Herald*

"You'll be engrossed by McBain's fast, lean prose." —*Chicago Tribune*

"McBain redefines the American police novel...he can stop you dead in your tracks with a line of dialogue." —*Cleveland Plain Dealer*

"The wit, the pacing, his relish for the drama of human diversity [are] what you remember about McBain novels." —*Philadelphia Inquirer*

"McBain is a top pro, at the top of his game." —*Los Angeles Daily News*

LADY KILLER

LADY KILLER

AN 87TH PRECINCT NOVEL

ED M^CBAIN

THOMAS & MERCER

Text copyright ©1958 Ed McBain
Republished in 2011

Printed in the United States of America.

Published by Thomas & Mercer
P.O. Box 400818
Las Vegas, NV 89140

ISBN-13: 9781612181738
ISBN-10: 1612181732

The city in these pages is imaginary.
The people, the places are all fictitious.
Only the police routine is based on established
investigatory technique.

INTRODUCTION

Lady Killer was written in nine days during the summer of 1957. My records show that I was paid the delivery advance on August 2 of that year, so I'm assuming I delivered the book sometime in July.

We were renting a house on Martha's Vineyard that summer, and I wanted to get the book out of the way as soon as possible so I could go flop on the beach. I set myself up in a garage behind the house and worked straight through for nine days, twenty pages a day, which came to 180 manuscript pages. No rewrites. Play it as it lays.

The 87th Precinct novels were still paperback originals in those days, and that was the required length—180. Not a page more, not a page less. If they'd been as long as today's 87th Precinct novels, which run some 400 to 450 pages in manuscript, I'd have been in that damn garage all summer.

Twenty pages a day was not unusual for me back then. This output diminished over the years to ten pages a day, and eventually to eight pages a day, which is about my current speed. Critics seem to believe that fast is lousy. That's because it takes them a week and a half to write a 400-word book review praising a novel somebody took seventeen years to write. The odd thing about *Lady Killer* is that it is no better and no worse than any of the 87th Precinct novels over which I labored longer. This may mean that *all* of them are lousy.

On the morning of the ninth day, Sloan Wilson and his family arrived.

I'm sure you remember the author of *The Man in the Gray Flannel Suit* and *A Summer Place*, among other worthy novels. We had invited him and his then wife Elise and their three children to spend a week with us—but who expected them to arrive while I was about to jump into the last twenty pages of a book? Well, actually, *we'd* expected them to arrive, since that was the date we'd put on the calendar. So here they were, ready to go swimming and bicycling and sunning and fishing and whatnot while I was ready to walk over to the garage. Talk about suspense.

You must understand that I was used to children running around underfoot while I was writing. My own three sons were respectively seven and five and five that summer—two of them were twins. But here were three *more* kids ranging in age and size from smaller to taller, ready for a whole week of fun in the sun and not understanding at all—even though their own *father* was a writer—that a murderer was waiting in the garage. Sloan knew all about deadlines, though, even self-inflicted ones, and he offered to take my eldest son and his own son fishing while the women went to the beach with the other children and I went to finish my book.

There I was, alone in the garage.

It was around 4:00 in the afternoon when everyone came back to the house. I was on the last few pages of the book, closing in on the killer. But here came Sloan and the boys, and the two women, and my twins, and the two girls, and there was such a commotion over at the house that I thought someone was being murdered over *there*, never mind the garage.

What happened was they'd caught a shark.

Well, I tell you!

None of us but Sloan had ever eaten shark meat, who claimed it was delicious and insisted that he prepare it for dinner. My son's expression said *Boy*, Dad, *you* never caught a shark, *you* never ate a shark, *you* don't know how to cook a shark, *you* never sliced open a shark's belly the way Mr. Wilson is doing right this minute before my very own eyes! Like sous chef and grand master, they puttered and pattered about the kitchen, finally carrying fillets to the skillet on the stove, where together they began frying up a fine smelly mess of fish. I went back to see how my people in the garage were doing.

They were doing okay.

The book is okay, too, I think.

In fact, I kind of like it.

Because I was driven by a singular need to get onto the beach as soon as possible, the book itself is driven by a single plot. It's a no-frills book. You jump right into it, you move right along with it, you let it take you where it wants to go. And because it was written fast, it seems to *move* fast. The ticking twelve-hour clock in the book seems to echo the urgency of the deadline I'd set for myself. Nine days. Twenty pages a day. Clocks are ticking and the cotton is high.

Speaking of Cotton, you'll notice that in this book I simply had no time to fool around with making Hawes a big *S*T*A*R*, the way a misguided publishing person had earlier insisted. Instead, he becomes a mere human being, an integral part of other humans in the repertory company of cops. I like him better this way.

It took more time to get the stench of that damn shark out of the kitchen than it did to write this book.

—ED McBAIN
NORWALK, CONNECTICUT
FEBRUARY 1994

WERE YOU
A CRANK
T H I S WEEK????

A crank is a person who calls Frederick 7-8024 and says, "I don't want to have to tell you about that Chinese laundry downstairs again. The owner uses a steam iron, and the hissing keeps me awake. Now, will you please arrest him?"

A crank is a person who addresses a letter to the 87th Precinct and writes: "I am surrounded by assassins. I need police protection. The Russians know that I have invented a supersonic tank."

Every police precinct in the world gets its share of crank calls and letters every day of the week. The calls and letters range from the sincere to the idiotic to the sublime. There are people who have information about suspected Communists, kidnapers, murderers, abortionists, forgers, and high-class whorehouses. There are people who complain about television comedians, mice, landlords, loud phonographs, strange ticking sounds in the walls, and automobile horns that play, "I'll be down to getya inna taxi, honey." There are people who claim to have been exhorted, extorted, duped, threatened, libeled, slandered, beaten, maimed, and even murdered. The classic call at the 87th was from a woman who claimed to have been shot dead four days ago, and why hadn't the police yet found her murderer?

There are, too, mysterious and anonymous calls that flatly and simply state, "There is a bomb in a shoe box at the Avon Theater." Crank calls can be terrifying. Crank calls and letters cost the city a lot of time and expense. The trouble is, you see, that you can't tell a crank from a non-crank without a program.

```
        WERE YOU
        A CRANK
     THIS WEEK????
```

It was Wednesday, July 24.

The city was hot, and the muster room of the 87th Precinct was probably the hottest place in the city. Dave Murchison sat behind the high desk to the left of the entrance doorway and wished that his underwear shorts would stop riding up his buttocks. It was only 8:00 in the morning, but the city had been building a blast-oven temperature all the preceding day, and the night had brought no relief. And now, with the sun barely up, the city was still wilted. It was difficult to imagine any further wilting, but Dave Murchison knew the muster room would get hotter and hotter and hotter as the day wore on, and he knew the small rotating fan on the corner of the high desk would not help to cool the room, and he also knew his undershorts would continue to ride up his buttocks.

At 7:45 A.M., Captain Frick, the commanding officer of the precinct, had inspected the handful of uniformed policemen who had not relieved their colleagues on post. He had then sent them out into the streets and turned Murchison.

"Going to be a scorcher, huh, Dave?" he had asked.

Murchison had nodded bleakly. He was fifty-three years old and had lived through many a suffocating summer in his day. He had learned over the years that comments about the weather very rarely changed the weather. The thing to do was sit it out quietly. It was his own belief that all this heat was caused by those damn H-bomb explosions in the Pacific. Human beings had begun messing around with stuff best left to God, and this was what they got for it.

Surlily, Dave Murchison tugged at his underwear.

He barely looked at the boy who mounted the stone steps before the station house and walked into the muster room. The kid glanced at the sign requesting all visitors to stop at the desk. He walked to the sign and stood before it, laboriously working out the words.

"What do you want, sonny?" Murchison asked.

"You the desk sergeant?"

"I'm the desk sergeant," Murchison said. He reflected on the virtues of a job that made it necessary to justify yourself to a snotnose.

"Here," the kid said, and he handed Murchison an envelope. Murchison took it. The boy started out of the building.

"Just a second, kid," Murchison said.

The kid didn't stop. He kept walking, down the steps, out onto the sidewalk, into the city, into the world.

"Hey!" Murchison said. Hastily, he looked around him for a patrolman. He had never seen it to fail. There never was a cop around when you needed one.

Sourly, he tugged at his undershorts and opened the envelope. He read the single page inside the envelope. Then he folded the page, put it back into the envelope, and shouted, "Is there another damn cop in this building besides me?"

A patrolman poked his head from behind one of the doors on the ground floor.

"Something wrong, Sarge?" he asked.

"Where the hell *is* everybody?"

"Around," the patrolman said. "We're around."

"Take this letter up to the squadroom," Murchison said. He handed the envelope over the desk.

"A *billet-doux*?" the patrolman asked. Murchison did not reply. It was too hot for half-assed attempts at humor. The patrolman shrugged and followed the pointing DETECTIVE DIVISION sign to the second floor of the building.

He walked down the corridor, stopped at the slatted-rail divider, pushed open the gate in the railing, walked to the desk of Cotton Hawes, and said, "Desk sergeant said to bring this up here."

"Thanks," Hawes said, and he opened the letter.

The letter read:

Detective Hawes read the letter and then read it again. His first reaction was "Crank."

His second reaction was "Suppose not?"

Sighing, he shoved back his chair and walked across the squadroom. He was a tall man, six feet two inches in slipper socks, and he weighed 190 pounds. He had blue eyes and a square jaw with a cleft chin. His hair was red, except for a streak over his left temple where he had once been knifed and where the hair had curiously grown in white after the wound healed. His straight nose was clean and unbroken, and he had a good mouth with a wide lower lip. His fists were huge. He used one of them now on the lieutenant's door.

"Come!" Lieutenant Byrnes shouted.

Hawes opened the door and stepped into the corner office. A rotating fan swept air across the lieutenant's desk. Byrnes sat behind the desk, a compact man in shirtsleeves, his tie pulled down, his collar open, the sleeves rolled up over his biceps.

"The newspapers say rain," he said. "Where the hell's the rain?" Hawes grinned. "You bringing me trouble, Hawes?"

"I don't know. What do you think?" He put the letter on Byrnes's desk.

Byrnes read it rapidly. "It never fails," he said. "We always get the cuckoos when the temperature's in the nineties. It drives them out of the woodwork."

"Do you think it's a crank, sir?"

"How the hell do I know? It's either a crank, or it's legit." He smiled. "That's a phenomenal bit of deduction, isn't it? It's no wonder I'm a lieutenant."

"What do we do?" Hawes asked.

"What time is it?"

Hawes looked at his watch. "A little past eight, sir."

"That gives us about twelve hours—assuming this is legit—to stop a potential killer from knocking off 'the lady,' whoever she is. Twelve hours to find a killer and a victim in a city of eight million people, with nothing more to go on than this letter. If it's legit."

"It may be, sir."

"I know," Byrnes said reflectively. "It may also be somebody's idea of a joke. Nothing to do? Time growing heavy on your hands? Write a letter to the cops. Send them off on a wild-goose chase. It could be that, Cotton."

"Yes, sir."

"Don't you think it's time you started calling me Pete?"

"Yes, sir."

Byrnes nodded. "Who's handled this letter, outside of you and me?"

"The desk sergeant, I imagine. I didn't touch the surface, sir… Pete…if you're thinking of latents."

"I am," Byrnes said. "Who's on the desk?"

"Dave Murchison."

"He's a good man, but I'll bet his prints are all over this damn thing. How was he to know what was inside the envelope?" Byrnes thought for a moment. "Let's play it safe, Cotton. When we send this over to the lab, we'll shoot a copy of your prints, mine, and Dave's with it. It might save Grossman's boys a lot of time. Time looks like the one thing we can use."

"Yes, sir," Hawes said.

Byrnes picked up his phone, pressed the intercom button twice, and waited.

"Captain Frick," a voice answered.

"John, this is Pete," Byrnes said. "Can you—"

"Hello, Pete," Frick said. "Going to be a scorcher, huh?"

"Yeah," Byrnes said. "John, can you relieve Murchison at the desk for an hour or so?"

"I suppose so. Why?"

"And get a man set up with the roller and pad. I want some prints taken right now."

"Who'd you pick up, Pete?"

"Nobody."

"Well, whose prints do you want?"

"Mine, Hawes's, and Murchison's."

"Oh, I see," Frick said, completely bewildered.

"I'll need a squad car with a siren and a man you can spare. I'll also want to question Murchison."

"You sound pretty mysterious, Pete. Want to—"

"We're coming down now to get printed," Byrnes said. "Will you be ready for us?"

"Sure, sure," Frick said, mystified.

"Bye, John."

The three men were printed.

The prints and the letter were put together into a large manila envelope, and the package was entrusted to a patrolman. The patrolman was instructed to drive directly to Headquarters downtown on High Street, using his siren all the way. He would deliver the package to Sam Grossman, the lieutenant in charge of the police laboratory there, and then he would wait while Sam's men photographed the letter. He would bring the photograph back to the 87th, where the detectives would study it while Grossman's laboratory technicians performed their various tests on the original. Grossman had already been called and informed that speed was essential. The patrolman knew this, too. When the squad car pulled away from the curb in front of the station house, the tires were squealing and the siren was beginning its high wail.

Inside the precinct, in the detective squadroom, a cop named Dave Murchison was being questioned by Byrnes and Hawes.

"Who delivered the letter, Dave?"

"A kid," Murchison said.

"Boy or girl?"

"Boy."

"How old?"

"I don't know. Ten? Eleven? Somewhere around there."

"What color hair?"

"Blond."

"Eyes?"

"I didn't notice."

"How tall?"

"Average height for a kid that age."

"What was he wearing?"

"Dungarees and a striped T-shirt."

"What color stripes?"

"Red."

"That ought to be easy," Hawes said.

"Any hat?" Byrnes asked.

"No."

"What kind of shoes?"

"I didn't see his feet from behind the desk."

"What did he say to you?"

"He asked if I was the desk sergeant. I told him I was. He handed me the letter."

"Did he say who it was from?"

"No. He just handed it to me and said, 'Here.'"

"What then?"

"He walked out."

"Why didn't you stop him?"

"I was alone with the desk, sir. I yelled for him to stop, but he didn't. I couldn't leave the desk, and nobody else was around."

"What about the desk lieutenant?"

"Frank was having a cup of coffee. I couldn't stick with the switchboard and also go chasing a kid."

"Okay, Dave, don't get excited."

"I mean, what the hell, Frank wants a cup of coffee, that's his business. He only went upstairs to Clerical. How the hell were we supposed to know this would happen?"

"Don't get excited, Dave."

"I'm not excited. I'm just saying there was nothing wrong with Frank getting a cup of coffee, that's all. In this heat you got to make allowances. A man sits behind that desk, he begins to—"

"Okay, Dave, okay."

"Look, Pete," Murchison said, "I'm sorry as hell. If I'd known this kid was going to be important—"

"It's all right, Dave. Did you handle the letter much?"

Murchison looked at the floor. "The letter and the envelope both. I'm sorry, Pete. I didn't think this would be—"

"It's all right, Dave. When you get back to the switchboard, turn on your radio, will you? Give a description of this kid to all the cars in the precinct. Get one car to cruise and alert every foot patrolman. I want the kid brought in as soon as he's located."

"Right," Murchison said. He looked at Byrnes. "Pete, I'm sorry if I—"

Byrnes clapped him on the shoulder. "Forget it," he said. "Get those calls out, will you?"

The maximum pay for a patrolman in the city that cradled the 87th Precinct was $5,015 a year. That is not a lot of money. In addition to that $5,015, the patrolman received $125 for the annual maintenance of his uniforms. That is still not a lot of money.

It becomes even less money when the various deductions are made every two weeks on payday. Four bucks comes out automatically for hospitalization, and another buck and a half is deducted for the precinct bed tax. This tax pays the salary of police widows who make up the dozen or so precinct beds that are used in emergencies when two shifts are on duty—and that are sometimes used by anyone wanting to catch a little shut-eye, emergency or no. Federal income tax takes another bite. The Police Benevolent Association, a sort of union for the law enforcers, gets its cut. The *High Street Journal*, the police publication, is usually subscribed to, hence another bite. If the cop has been decorated, he donates to the Police Honor Legion. If he's religious, he donates to the various societies and the various charities that visit the precinct each year. His paycheck, after it has been divided and subdivided, usually comes to $130 every two weeks.

That amounts to sixty-five bucks a week no matter how you slice it.

If some cops take graft—and some cops *do* take graft—it may be because they're slightly hungry.

A police force is a small army, and as with any military organization, the orders must be obeyed no matter how ridiculous they may sound. When the foot patrolmen and the radio motor patrolmen of the 87th received their orders that morning of July 24, they thought the orders were rather peculiar. Some shrugged. Some cursed. Some simply nodded. All obeyed.

The orders were to pick up a ten-year-old boy with blond hair who was wearing dungarees and a red-striped T-shirt.

It sounded simple.

At 9:15 A.M. the photograph of the letter came back from the lab. Byrnes called a meeting in his office. He put the letter in the center of his desk, and he and three other detectives studied it.

"What do you make of it, Steve?" he asked. He asked Steve Carella first because of many reasons. To begin with, he thought Carella was the best cop on his squad. True, Hawes was beginning to shape up, even though he'd made a bad start shortly after his transfer to the precinct. But Hawes, in Byrnes's estimation, had a long way to go before he would equal Carella. Secondly, and quite apart from the fact that Carella was a good cop and a tough cop, Brynes felt personally attached to him. He would never forget that Carella had risked his life, and almost lost it, trying to crack a case in which Byrnes's son had been involved. In Byrnes's mind, Carella had become almost a *second* son. And so, like any father with a son in the business, he asked for Carella's opinion first.

"I've got my own theories about guys who send letters like this," Carella said. He picked up the photograph and held it to the light streaming through the windows. He was a tall, deceptively slender man, giving an impression of strength without the slightest hint of massive power. His eyes were slightly slanted and together with his clean-shaven look, they gave him a high-cheeked, somewhat-Oriental appearance.

"What's your idea, Steve?" Byrnes asked.

Carella tapped the photograph. "The first question I ask is why? If this joker is about to commit homicide, he sure as hell knows there are laws against it. The obvious way to do murder is to do it secretly and quietly and try to escape the law. But no. He sends us a letter. Why does he send us a letter?"

"It's more fun for him this way," said Hawes, who had been listening intently to Carella. "He's got a double challenge—the challenge of killing someone and the challenge of getting away with it after he's raised the odds."

"That's one way to look at it," Carella said, and Byrnes watched the interplay between the two cops and was pleased by it. "But there's another possibility. He *wants* to get caught."

"Like this Heirens kid in Chicago, a few years back?" Hawes said.

"Sure. The lipstick on the mirror. Catch me before I kill again." Carella tapped the letter. "Maybe *he* wants to get caught, too. Maybe he's scared stiff of killing and wants us to catch him before he *has* to kill. What do you think, Pete?"

Byrnes shrugged. "It's a theory. In any case, we still have to catch him."

"I know, I know," Carella said. "But if he wants to get caught, then the letter isn't just a letter. Do you follow me?"

"No."

Detective Meyer nodded. "I get you, Steve. He's not just warning us, He's tipping us."

"Sure," Carella said. "If he wants to get caught, if he wants to be stopped, this letter'll tell us just how to stop him. It'll tell us who and where." He dropped the letter on Byrnes's desk.

Detective Meyer walked over to it and studied it. Meyer was a very patient cop, and so his scrutiny of the letter was careful and slow. Meyer, you see, had a father who was something of a practical joker. The senior Meyer, whose name was Max, had been somewhat startled and surprised when his wife had announced she was going to have a change-of-life baby. When the baby had been born, Max had played his little joke on humanity and incidentally on his son. He had given the baby the name of Meyer, which added to the surname of Meyer, had caused the infant to emerge as Meyer Meyer. The joke had doubtless been a masterpiece of hilarity. Except perhaps to Meyer Meyer. The boy had grown up as an Orthodox Jew in a predominantly Gentile neighborhood. The kids on the block had been accustomed to taking out their petty hatreds on scapegoats, and what better scapegoat than one whose name presented a ready-made chant: "Meyer Meyer, Jew-on-Fire!" In all fairness, they had never put Meyer Meyer to the stake. But he had suffered many a beating in the days of his youth, and faced with what seemed to be the overwhelming odds of life, he had developed an attitude of extreme patience toward his fellow man.

Patience is an exacting virtue. Perhaps Meyer Meyer had emerged unscarred and unscathed. Perhaps. He was nonetheless completely bald. There are a lot of men who are completely bald. But Meyer Meyer was only thirty-seven years old.

Patiently, exactingly, he studied the letter now.

"It doesn't say a hell of a lot, Steve," he said.

"Read it," Byrnes told him.

"'I will kill The Lady tonight at eight,'" Meyer quoted. "'What can you do about it?'"

"Well, it tells us who," Carella said.

"Who?" Byrnes asked.

"'The Lady,'" Carella said.

"And who's she?"

"I don't know."

"Mmmm."

"It doesn't tell us how," Meyer said, "or where."

"But it does give a time," Hawes put in.

"Eight. Tonight at eight."

"You really think this character wants to get caught, Steve?"

"I really don't know. I'm just offering a theory. I do know one thing."

"What's that?"

"Until we get a report from the lab, we'd better start with what we've got."

Byrnes looked at the letter.

"Well, what the hell do we have?"

"The Lady," Carella answered.

Fats Donner was a stool pigeon.

There are stool pigeons and there are stool pigeons, and there is no law in the city that prevents you from getting your information from whomever you want to. If you like Turkish baths, there is no better stool pigeon than Fats.

When Hawes had worked with the 30th Squad, he had had his own coterie of informers. Unfortunately, his tattletales had all been highly specialized men who were hip only to the crimes and criminals within the 30th Precinct. Their limited scope did not extend to the brawling, sprawling 87th. And so, at 9:27 A.M. that morning, while Steve Carella went to see his own preferred stoolie—a man named Danny Gimp—and while Meyer Meyer checked the Lousy File for any female criminals who might have used "The Lady" as an alias, Cotton Hawes spoke to Detective Hal Willis, and Willis told him to look up Donner.

A call to Donner's apartment drew a blank.

"He's probably at the baths," Willis said, and he gave Hawes the address. Hawes checked out a car and drove downtown.

The sign outside the place read:

REGAN BATHS
Turkish
Steam
Galvanized

Hawes walked in, climbed a flight of wooden steps leading to the second floor of the building, and stopped before a desk in the lobby. The climb had already brought perspiration to Hawes's forehead. He wondered why anyone would go to a Turkish bath on a day like today, and then he further wondered why anyone would go swimming in January, and then he thought the hell with it.

"What can I do you for?" the man at the desk asked. He was a small man with a sharp nose. He wore a white T-shirt upon which the name REGAN BATHS was stenciled in green. He also wore a green eyeshade.

"Police," Hawes said, and he flashed the tin.

"You got the wrong place," the man said. "This is a legit bath. Somebody steered you wrong."

"I'm looking for a man named Fats Donner. Know where I can find him?"

"Sure," the man said. "Donner's a regular. You got no beef with me?"

"Who are you?"

"Alf Regan. I run the joint. Legit."

"I only want to talk to Donner. Where is he?"

"Room 4, middle of the hall. You can't go in like that, mister."

"What do I need?"

"Just your skin. But I'll give you a towel. Lockers are back there. Anything valuable, you can leave here at the desk. I'll put it in the safe."

Hawes unloaded his wallet and watch. He debated for a moment, and then unclipped his service revolver and holster and put them on the desk.

"That thing loaded?" Regan asked.

"Yes."

"Mister, you better—"

"It's got an internal safety," Hawes said. "It can't go off unless the trigger is pulled."

Regan looked at the .38 skeptically. "Okay, okay," he said, "but I wonder how many people accidentally get shot by guns that got internal safeties."

Hawes grinned and headed for the lockers. While he was undressing, Regan brought him a towel.

"I hope you got a thick hide," he said.

"Why?"

"Donner likes them hot. I mean *hot.*"

Hawes wrapped the towel around his middle.

"You got a good build," Regan said. "Ever do any boxing?"

"A little."

"Where?"

"In the Navy."

"Any good?"

"Fair."

"Take a punch," Regan said.

"What?"

"Throw a punch at me."

"What for?"

"Go ahead, go ahead."

"I'm in a hurry," Hawes said.

"Just take a swing. I want to see something." Regan put up his hands in a fighting stance.

Hawes shrugged, feinted with his left, and then crossed a right at Regan's jaw, pulling the punch just before it hammered home.

"Why'd you pull it?" Regan demanded.

"I didn't want to knock your head off."

"Who taught you that feint?"

"A lieutenant j.g. named Bohan."

"He taught you good. I manage a couple of fighters on the side. You ever think of going into the ring?"

"Never."

"Think about it. This country could use a heavyweight champ."

"I'll think about it," Hawes said.

"You'd make a hell of a lot more than the city pays you, you can bet your ass on that. Even doing tankers, you'd make a hell of a lot more."

"Well, I'll think about it," Hawes said. "Where's Donner?"

"Down the hall. Listen, take my card. You ever decide to take a whack at it, give me a ring. Who knows? Maybe we got another Dempsey here, huh?"

"Sure," Hawes said. He took the card Regan offered him and then looked down at the towel. "Where do I put the card?" he asked.

"Oh. Oh, yeah. Well, give it to me. I'll catch you on the way out. Donner's right down the hall. Room 4. You can't miss it. There's enough steam in there to move the *Queen Mary*."

Hawes started down the corridor. He passed a thin man who looked at him suspiciously. The man was naked, and his suspicion was bred by the towel Hawes wore. Hawes passed the man guiltily, feeling very much like a photographer in a nudist colony. He found Room 4, opened the door, and was hit in the face by a blast

of heat that almost sent him reeling back down the corridor. He tried to see through the layers of shifting steam in the room, but it was impossible.

"Donner?" he called.

"Here, man," a voice answered.

"Where?"

"Over here, man. Sittin'. Who is it?"

"My name's Cotton Hawes. I work on Hal Willis's squad. He told me to contact you."

"Oh, yeah. Come on in, man, come on in," the bodiless voice said. "Close the door. You're lettin' steam out and drafts in."

Hawes closed the door. If he had ever wondered how a loaf of bread feels when the oven door seals it in, he now knew. He worked his way across the room. The heat was suffocating. He tried to suck air into his lungs, found only heat passing into his throat. A figure suddenly materialized in the shifting hot fog.

"Donner?" Hawes asked.

"Ain't nobody here but us chickens, boss," Donner answered, and Hawes grinned despite the heat.

Fats was truly fat in the plural. He was citywide, he was statewide, he was continental. Like a giant, quivering bowl of white flesh, he sat on the marble bench against the wall, languishing in the fetid air, a towel draped across his crotch. Each time he breathed, layers of fat shook and trembled.

"You're a cop, ain't you?" he asked Hawes.

"Sure."

"You said Willis's squad, but that coulda meant like other things. Willis gave me the nod, huh?"

"Yes," Hawes said.

"Good man, Willis. I saw him dump a guy who musta weighed four hundred pounds right on his ass. Judo. He's a judo expert. You reach for him and *push-pull-click-click!* your arm's in a plaster cast. Man, we in danger." Donner chuckled. When he chuckled, everything he owned chuckled with him. The motion was making Hawes a little seasick.

"So what do you want to know?" Donner asked.

"Know anybody called 'The Lady'?" Hawes said, figuring it was best to come straight to the point before he collapsed of heat prostration.

"The Lady," Donner said. "Fancy handle. She in the rackets?"

"Maybe."

"I knew a dame called 'The Lady Bird' in St. Louis. She was a stoolie. Damn good one, too. So they called her The Lady Bird. Pigeon, bird, you dig?"

"I dig," Hawes said.

"She knew everything, but everything, man, everything! You know how she got the dope?"

"I can imagine," Hawes said.

"Well, it don't take much imagination. That's exactly how she got it. She could get information from the Sphinx, I swear to God. Right in the middle of the desert, she'd—"

"She's not in this city, is she?"

"No. She's dead. She got information from a guy it was very unhealthy to get information from. An occupational hazard. Bam! No more Lady Bird."

"He killed her because she stooled on him?"

"That, and also one other thing. Like it seems she also gave him the clap. This guy was a very clean fellow, personal habits, I mean. He didn't appreciate what she give him. Bam! No more Lady Bird." Donner thought for a moment. "Come to think of it, she wasn't such a lady, huh?"

"I guess not. What about the lady we want?"

"You got a hint?"

"She's going to be killed tonight."

"Yeah? Who's gonna kill her?"

"That's what we're trying to find out."

"Mmm. A tough nut, huh?"

"Yeah. Listen, do you think we could step outside and talk there?"

"What's the matter? You got a chill? I can ask them to turn up the—"

"No, no, no," Hawes said hastily.

"The Lady, huh?" Donner asked, thinking. "The Lady."

"Yes."

It seemed to be getting hotter. While Donner sat and thought, the temperature in the room seemed to mount steadily. Each second of thought seemed to bring a corresponding second of increased heat. Hawes was gulping in air through his mouth, gasping for breath. He wanted to take off the towel, wanted to take of his skin and hang it on a peg. He wanted a glass of ice-cold water He wanted a glass of cool water. He would accept a glass of lukewarm water. He'd settle for hot water, which, he was certain, would be cooler than the temperature of the room. Sweating from every pore, he sat while Donner thought. The seconds ticked by. The perspiration trickled down his face, poured from his wide shoulders, streamed down his backbone.

"There was a colored dancer at the old Black and White Club," Donner said.

"She around now?"

"No, she does a strip in Miami. They called her 'The Lady.' She did a very delicate strip. For those who got the Shy Young Thing Fetish combined with the Colored Fetish. She was a big hit. But she's in Miami now."

"Who's here?"

"I'm trying to think," Donner said.

"Can you think a little faster?"

"I'm thinking, I'm thinking," Donner said. "There was a pusher called 'The Lady.' But I think she went to New York. That's where all the junkie money is these days. Yeah, she's in New York."

"Well, who's here?" Hawes asked irritably, wiping his sweaty face with a sweaty hand.

"Hey, I know," Donner said.

"Who?"

"The Lady. A new hooker on Whore Street. You familiar?"

"Vaguely."

"She works for Mama Ida. You know the place?"

"No."

"The boys on the squad will. Look her up. The Lady. At Mama Ida's."

"Do you know her?" Hawes asked.

"The Lady? Only professionally."

"Whose profession? Yours or hers?"

"Mine. I got some info from her a couple of weeks back. Jesus, I shoulda thought of her right away. Only I never call her 'The Lady.' That's for the trade. Her real name is Marcia. She's a peacheroo."

"Tell me about her."

"Not much to tell. You want the straight story or the story on the Street? I mean, you want to know about Marcia—or about The Lady?"

"Both."

"Okay. Here's the way Mama Ida tells it. She's parlayed this thing into a fortune, believe me. Anybody comes down to the Street, they look for Mama Ida's joint. And once they find it, they're itching to tackle The Lady."

"Why?"

"Because Mama Ida's got a good imagination. Here's the legend. Marcia was born in Italy. She's the daughter of some Italian count who's got a villa on the Mediterranean. During the war, Marcia—against the wishes of her father—married a guerrilla who was fighting Mussolini. She took about ten thousand dollars in jewels with her and went to live in the hills with him. Picture this flower of nobility, a kid who knew how to ride before she knew how to walk, living in a cave with a band of bearded men. Well, one day her husband got killed in a raid on a railroad. Second in command claimed Marcia as his own, and pretty soon the entire band of cutthroats was getting in on the act. One night Marcia took off. They chased her through the hills, but she escaped.

"Her jewels bought her passage to America. But she was an enemy alien and had to stay in hiding. Barely able to speak the language, unable to get a job, she drifted into prostitution. She's still in the racket, but she loathes it. Goes about it in a ladylike fashion, and every time she's had, it's like rape. That's The Lady, and that's the way Mama Ida tells it."

"What's the real story?" Hawes asked.

"Her name's Marcia Polenski. She's from Scranton. She's been a hooker since she was sixteen, has the shrewdness of a viper, and a good ear for dialect. The Italian accent is as phony as the rape scenes."

"Any enemies?" Hawes asked.

"How do you mean?"

"Anybody who'd want to kill her?"

"Probably every other hooker on the Street wants to kill her. But I doubt if any of them would."

"Why?"

"Hookers are nice people. I like them."

"Well," Hawes said noncommittally. He rose. "I'm getting out of here."

"Will Willis take care of me?" Donner asked.

"Yeah. Talk to him about it. So long," Hawes said hastily. "Thanks."

"*De nada*," Donner replied, and he leaned against the steam.

After Hawes had dressed and listened to a dissertation by Regan on the big money to be made in boxing, accompanied by Regan's card and an admonition to keep it in a safe place, he went out into the street and called the squad. He got Carella.

"You back?" he asked.

"Yeah. I was waiting for your call."

"What'd you get?"

"Danny Gimp tells me there's a hooker named The Lady working on the Street. She may be our baby."

"I got the same from Donner," Hawes said.

"Good. Let's look her up. This may turn out to be simpler than we thought."

"Maybe so," Hawes said. "Want me to come back to the squad?"

"No, I'll meet you on the Street. Jenny's, do you know it?"

"I'll find it," Hawes said.

"What time have you got?"

Hawes looked at his watch. "Ten-o-three," he said.

"Can you meet me at ten-fifteen?"

"I'll be there," Hawes said, and he hung up.

La Vía de Putas was a street in Isola that ran north and south for a total of three blocks. Over the course of years, the street had changed its name many times, but never its profession. It had changed its name only to accommodate the incoming immigrant groups, translating "Whore Street" into as many languages as there were nations. The profession, as solidly economic a profession as undertaking, had steadfastly defied the buffetings of time, tide, and policemen. In fact, the policemen were, in a sense, part of the profession. Whore Street, you see, was not a secret. Trying to keep the Street a secret would have been like trying to keep the existence of Russia a secret. There was hardly a citizen, and barely a visitor, who had not heard of La Vía de Putas, and many citizens had firsthand knowledge of the practices plied there. And if the citizenry know of something, the police—as slow-witted as they sometimes are—know of it, too.

It was here that the oldest profession clasped hands with the neophyte profession. And during the clasping of hands, bills of various denominations were exchanged so that the Street could continue its brisk trade without interference from the Law. Things got difficult for the 87th's cops when the Vice Squad decided to get puritanical. But even then, it didn't take cops long to realize that the green stuff could be divided and then subdivided. There was plenty of it to go all the way around, and there was certainly no reason to get stuffy about something as universal as sex.

Besides, and here was rationalization of the most sublime sort, was it not better to have most of the precinct's hookers contained in an area three blocks long rather than scattered all over the streets? Of course it was. Crime was something like information for a thesis. So long as you knew where to find it, you were halfway home.

The uniformed cops of the 87th knew where to find it—and they also knew how to lose it. Every now and then they would stop by and chat with the various Mamas who ran the brothels. Mama Luz, Mama Theresa, Mama Carmen, Mama Ida, Mama Inez (from the song of the same name) were all bona fide madams and could all be counted on for the discreet payoff. In turn, the cops looked the other way. Sometimes, on a sleepy afternoon when the streets were quiet, they dropped into the cribs for a cup of coffee and things. The madams didn't mind too much. After all, if you ran a pushcart you expected the cop on the beat to take an apple every now and then, didn't you?

The detectives of the 87th rarely got a piece of the long green that shuttled from customer to hooker to madam to patrolman. The detectives had bigger things going for them, and everybody has to eat. Besides, they knew the Vice Squad was getting its cut, and they didn't want the pie sliced too many ways lest the bakery close shop altogether. Out of professional courtesy, they, too, looked the other way.

On Wednesday, July 24, at 10:21 A.M., Carella and Hawes looked the other way. Jenny's was a tiny dump on the corner of Whore Street. Most of the payoffs took place in Jenny's, but Carella and Hawes were not looking for payoffs. They were discussing The Lady.

"From what I understand," Carella said, "we may have to wait in line to see her."

Hawes grinned. "Why don't you let me handle this one alone, Steve?" he said. "After all, you're a married man. I don't want to corrupt—"

"I've been corrupted," Carella said. He looked at his watch. "It isn't even ten-thirty yet. If this works out, we're nine and a half hours ahead of our killer."

"*If* it works out," Hawes said.

"Well, let's go see her." He paused. "You ever been in one of these joints?"

"We had a lot of high-class call houses in the 30th," Hawes said.

"These ain't high class, son," Carella said. "These are very low class. If you've got a clothespin, put it on your nose."

They paid their bill and went into the street. Halfway up the block, a radio motor patrol car was at the curb. Two patrolmen were on the sidewalk talking to a man and a woman, surrounded by kids.

"Trouble," Carella said. He quickened his pace. Hawes fell into step beside him.

"Now, take it easy," the patrolman was saying, "just take it easy!"

"Easy?" the woman shouted. "Why I should take it easy? This man—"

"Pipe down!" the second patrolman yelled. "You want the goddamn commissioner to drive up?"

Carella pushed his way through the knot of kids. He recognized the patrolmen at once, walked to the nearest one, and said, "What's up, Tom?"

The woman's face burst into a grin. "Stevie!" she said. "*Dio gracias.* Tell these stupids—"

"Hello, Mama Luz," Carella said.

The woman he addressed was a fat woman with alabaster-white skin and black hair pulled into a tight bun at the back of her neck. She wore a loose silk kimono, and her swelling bosom moved fluidly in the open neck. Her face was exquisitely carved, angelic, patrician. She was one of the most notorious madams in the entire city.

"What's up?" Carella asked the patrolman again.

"This guy don't want to pay," the patrolman said.

This guy was a little man in a seersucker suit. Standing alongside Mama Luz, he seemed thinner than he actually was. He had a small paintbrush mustache under his nose, and his black hair fell despondently onto his forehead.

"What do you mean?" Carella asked.

"He don't want to pay. He's been upstairs. Now he's tryin' to beat the check."

"Get *dinero* first, I always tell them," Mama Luz said, clucking. "*Dinero* first, then *amor.* No. This stupid, this new one, she forgets. So see what happens? Tell him, Stevie. Tell him I get my money."

"You're getting careless, Luz," Carella said.

"Yes, yes, I know. But tell him I get my money, Stevie. Tell this *Hitler!*"

Carella looked at the man, noticing the resemblance for the first time. The man had said nothing so far. With his arms folded across his chest, he stood beside Mama Luz, his lips pursed beneath the ridiculous paintbrush mustache, his eyes glaring heatedly.

"Are you a detective?" he asked suddenly.

"I am," Carella said.

"And you permit this sort of thing to go on in this city?"

"What sort of thing?" Carella asked.

"Open prostitution."

"I don't see any prostitution," Carella said.

"What are you, a pimp or something? A collection agency for every madam in the city?"

"Mister—" Carella started, and Hawes gently touched his arm. There was imminent danger in the situation, and Hawes recognized it immediately. It was one thing to look the other way. It was another thing to openly condone. Whatever Carella's relationship with Mama Luz, Hawes did not feel this was a time for him to be sticking his neck out. An irate call to Headquarters and there could be trouble, big trouble.

"We've got somebody to see, Steve," he said.

Carella's eyes met Hawes's and plainly asked him to keep the hell out of this.

"Were you upstairs, mister?" he asked the little man.

"Yes."

"Okay. I don't know what you did up there, and I'm not asking. That's your business. But I judge from that wedding band on your finger—"

The man pulled his hand back sharply.

"—that you wouldn't appreciate the idea of being hauled into court to testify on the open prostitution permitted in this city. I'm busy as hell, mister, so I'll leave the entire thing to your conscience. Come on, Cotton," he said.

He started up the street. Hawes caught up to him. As they walked, Hawes glanced over his shoulder.

"He's paying," he said.

Carella grunted.

"You sore?" Hawes asked.

"A little."

"I was only thinking of you."

"Mama Luz is a cooperative madam. Aside from that, I like her. Nobody asked that guy to come into the precinct. He came, he had a meal, and I think it's justice that he should pay for it. The girl he was with isn't in this for kicks. She works a hell of a lot harder than a five-and-dime clerk."

"Then why doesn't she become a five-and-dime clerk?" Hawes asked logically.

"*Touché*," Carella said, and he smiled. "Here's Mama Ida's."

Mama Ida's looked just like any of the other tenements lining the street. Two kids sat on the front stoop playing tic-tac-toe with a piece of chalk.

"Get off the stoop!" Carella said, and the kids scattered. "This is what burns me up," he said to Hawes. "The kids seeing all this. What a way to be brought up."

"A little while ago, you sounded as if you thought it was an honest profession," Hawes said.

"Are you looking for an argument?"

"No. I'm trying to find out what makes you tick."

"Okay. Crime isn't honest. Prostitution is crime, or at least it's crime in this city. Maybe the law's right, and maybe it isn't, and it's not for me to question it; it's only for me to enforce it. Okay. In this precinct, and maybe in every damn precinct, for all I know, prostitution is a crime that isn't a crime. Both those patrolmen are getting paid by every madam on the street. They keep trouble away from the madams, and the madams, in turn, run things clean. No muggings, no rollings. A clear act of commerce. But the guy who tried to cheat Luz was committing a crime, too, wasn't he? So where does the cop go from there? Does he turn his back on all crime or just some crimes?"

"No," Hawes said. "Only on the crimes for which he's been paid off."

Carella faced Hawes levelly. "I've never taken a dime all the time I've been on the force. Remember that."

"I didn't think you had."

"Okay," Carella said. "A cop can't do everything by the book. I've got a sense of right and wrong that has nothing whatever to do with the law. I thought Hitler was committing a wrong back there. No tickee, no shirtee. Basic. Maybe I stuck my neck out, maybe I didn't. I say it's Spam, and I say the hell with it."

"Okay," Hawes said.

"Are *you* sore now?"

"Nope. Just enlightened."

"There's one other thing," Carella said.

"What's that?"

"The kids surrounding that scene. Was it better to have them taking it all in? Or better to break it up?"

"You could have broken it up without forcing the guy to pay."

"You're a marksman today," Carella said, and they entered the building. Only one bell button in the hall panel worked. Carella rang it.

"Mama Ida's a bitch," he said. "She thinks she owns the street *and* the city. You've got to be rough with her."

The inside door opened. A woman with a hairbrush in her hand stood just inside the jamb. Her black hair was hanging loose around her face. The face was narrow, with piercing brown eyes. The woman wore a light-blue sweater and a black skirt. She was barefooted.

"What now?" she said.

"It's me. Carella. Let us in, Ida."

"What do you want, Carella? Are the bulls getting in the act now?"

"We want to see a girl you call 'The Lady.'"

"She's busy," Ida said.

"We'll wait."

"She may be a while."

"We'll wait."

"Wait outside."

"Ida," Carella said gently, "get the hell out of that doorway."

Ida moved back. Carella and Hawes stepped into a dim corridor.

"What do you want with her?" Ida asked.

"We want to ask her some questions."

"What about?"

"Police business," Carella answered.

"You're not going to take her away, are you?"

"No. Just some questions."

Ida smiled radiantly. There was a gold tooth at the front of her mouth. "Good," she said. "Come in. Sit down."

She led them into a small, cheerless parlor. There was the smell of incense in the room and the smell of perspiration. The perspiration won out.

Ida looked at Hawes. "Who's this one?" she asked.

"Detective Hawes," Carella said.

"Handsome," Ida said unenthusiastically. "What happened to your hair? How'd you get that white hair?"

"I'm getting old," Hawes said, touching the streak.

"How long will she be?" Carella asked.

"Who knows? She's slow. She's hard to get. She's The Lady, don't you know? Ladies have to be treated gently. Ladies have to be talked to."

"You must lose a lot of money with her."

"She costs three times more than the rest," Ida said.

"Is she worth it?"

She shrugged. "If you have to pay for it, I guess she's worth it." She looked at Hawes again. "I'll bet you never had to pay for it."

Hawes studied her blandly. He knew the woman was only talking in terms of her trade. He had never known a whore or a madam who did not discuss sex as simply as the average woman discussed clothes or babies. Nonetheless, he did not answer her.

"How old do you think I am?" she asked him.

"Sixty," he answered flatly.

Ida laughed. "You bastard," she said. "I'm only forty-five. Come around some afternoon."

"Thanks."

"Sixty," she scoffed. "I'll show you sixty."

Upstairs, a door opened and closed. There were footsteps in the hallway. Ida looked up.

"She's finished," she said.

A man came down the steps. He looked sheepishly into the parlor and then went out the front door.

"Come on," Ida said. She watched Hawes as he stood up. "A big one," she said, almost to herself, and then she led the detectives onto the stairway. "I really ought to charge you for her time."

"We can always take her to the squadroom," Carella said.

"I'm joking, Carella," Ida answered. "Don't you know when I'm joking? What's your first name, Hawes?"

"Cotton."

Doesn't your friend know when I'm joking, Cotton?" She paused on the steps and looked down at Hawes. "Are those sixty-year-old legs?" she asked.

"Seventy," Hawes answered, and Carella burst out laughing.

"You bastard," Ida said, but she could not suppress the chuckle that came to her throat. They passed into the upstairs corridor. In one of the rooms, a girl in a kimono was sitting on the edge of her bed, polishing her nails. The other doors along the corridor were closed. Ida went to one of the closed doors and knocked on it.

A soft voice answered, "*Si*? Who ees it?"

"Ida. Open up."

"One minute, *per piacere*."

Ida pulled a face and waited. The door opened. The girl standing in the doorframe was at least thirty-two years old. Black hair framed a tranquil face with deep-set brown eyes. There was sadness on the face and around the edges of the mouth. There was nobility in the way the girl held her head, in the way she kept her shoulders pulled back, one hand clutched daintily, protectively, to the neck of the kimono, holding it closed over the thrust of her breasts. There was fear in her eyes, as if she dreaded what was coming next.

"*Si*?" she said.

"Some gentlemen to see you," Ida said.

She looked to Ida plaintively. "Again?" she said. "Please, *signora*, not again I beg you. I am so—"

"Knock it off, Marcia," Ida said. "They're cops."

The fear left Marcia's eyes. The hand dropped from the neck of the kimono. The kimono fell open, revealing the first rise of her breasts. All nobility left her face and her carriage. There were hard lines about her eyes and her mouth.

"What's the beef?" she asked.

"None," Carella said. "We want to talk to you."

"You sure that's all?"

"That's all."

"Some cops come in here and expect—"

"Can it," Hawes said. "We want to talk."

"In here? Or downstairs?"

"Call your own shot."

"Here," she said. She stepped back. Carella and Hawes entered the room.

"You need me?" Ida asked.

"No."

"I'll be downstairs. Want a drink before you leave, Cotton?"

"No, thanks," Hawes said.

"What's the matter? You don't like me?" She cocked her head saucily. "I could show you a few things."

"I love you," Hawes said, grinning, and Carella looked at him in surprise. "I'm just afraid the exertion would kill you."

Mama Ida burst out laughing. "You bastard," she said, and she went out of the room. In the hallway he heard her mumble chucklingly, "The exertion would *kill* me!"

Marcia sat, crossing her legs in a most unladylike manner.

"Okay, what is it?" she asked.

"You been working here long?" Carella said.

"About six months."

"Get along?"

"I get along fine."

"Have any trouble since you've been here?"

"What do you mean?"

"Any arguments? Fights?"

"The usual. There's twelve girls here. Somebody's always yelling about using somebody else's bobby pins. You know how it is."

"How about anything serious?"

"Hair pulling? Like that?"

"Yes."

"No. I try to steer clear of the other girls. I get more money than they do, so they don't like it. I'm not looking for trouble. This is a cushy spot. Best I ever had it. Hell, I'm star of the show here." She pulled the kimono up over her knees. "Hot, ain't it?" she asked.

"Yes," Carella said. "Did you ever have any trouble with one of the customers?"

Marcia began flapping the kimono about her legs, using it as a fan. "What's this all about?" she asked.

"Did you?"

"Trouble with the customers? I don't know. Who the hell remembers? What's this all about?"

"We're trying to figure out whether or not somebody wants to kill you," Hawes said.

Marcia stopped fanning her legs with the kimono. The silk dropped from her fingers. "Come again," she said.

"You heard it the first time."

"*Kill* me? That's crazy. Who'd want to kill me?" She paused, then proudly added, "I'm a good lay."

"And you never had any trouble with a customer?"

"What kind of trouble could I—" She stopped. Her face went pensive. For a moment it took on the quiet nobility of her role as The Lady. When she spoke, the moment was gone. "You think it could be *him*?" she asked.

"What do you mean?"

"You're sure somebody wants to kill me? How do you know?"

"We don't know. We're guessing."

"Well, there was this guy..." She stopped. "Naw, he was just talking."

"Who?"

"Some jerk. A sailor. He kept trying to place me all the while he was here. Finally, he done it. Remembered me from New London. I was working there during the war. The submarine base, you know. Good pickings. He remembered me and claimed he got cheated, wanted his money back. Said I wasn't no Italian count's daughter, I was just a plain phony. I admitted I come from Scranton, but I told him he got what he paid for, and if he didn't like it, he could take a flying leap. He told me he'd come back. He said when he came back, he'd kill me."

"When was this?"

"About a month ago, I guess."

"Do you remember his name?"

"Yeah. I don't usually, except this guy raised a fuss. They all tell me their names, you know. First thing. Right off the bat. I'm Charlie, I'm Frank, I'm Ned. You'll remember me, won't you, honey? Remember them! Jesus! I have a hard enough time trying to *forget* some of them."

"But you remember this sailor, do you?"

"Sure. He said he was gonna kill me. Wouldn't you remember? Besides, he had a goofy name."

"What was it?"

"Mickey."

"Mickey what?"

"That's what I asked him. I said, 'What is it? Mickey Mouse?' It wasn't Mickey Mouse at all."

"What was it?"

"Mickey Carmichael. I can remember him saying it. Mickey Carmichael. Fire controlman second class. That's just the way he said it. As if he was saying, 'His Majesty, the king of England.' A nut. A real nut."

"Did he say where he was based?"

"He was on a ship. This was his first liberty in the city."

"Which ship?"

"I don't know. He called it a tin can. That's a battleship, ain't it?"

"That's a destroyer," Hawes said. "What else did he say about the ship?"

"Nothing. Except he was glad to be off it. Wait a minute. A strike? Something about a strike?"

"A striker?" Carella asked. He turned to Hawes. "That's a Navy term, isn't it?"

"Yes, but I don't see how it would apply to a noncommisioned officer. He *did* say Fire controlman second class, didn't he? He didn't say seaman second? Fire controlman striker?"

"No, no, he was a sergeant or something. He had red stripes on his sleeve."

"*Two* red stripes?"

"Yeah."

"He was a second-class petty officer," Hawes said. "She's right, Steve." He turned to the girl. "But he said something about a strike?"

"Something like that."

"A mutiny?"

"Something like that. A strike or something."

"A strike," Hawes said, half to himself. "Strikers, picket lines—" He snapped his fingers. "A picket! Did he say his ship was a picket ship?"

"Yeah," Marcia said, her eyes widening. "Yeah. That's exactly what he said. He seemed pretty proud of *that*, too."

"A picket destroyer," Hawes said. "That shouldn't give us much trouble. Mickey Carmichael." He nodded, "Anything else you want to ask her?"

"I'm finished."

"So am I. Thanks, miss."

"You think he's *really* gonna try to kill me?" Marcia asked.

"We'll find out," Hawes said.

"What should I do if he comes here?"

"We'll get to him before then."

"But suppose he gets past you?"

"He won't."

"I know. But suppose he does?"

"Try hiding under the bed," Carella said.

"Wise guy," Marcia said.

"We'll call you," Carella said. "If he's our man and you're his target, we'll let you know."

"Look, do me a favor. Let me know even if I *ain't*. I don't want to sit here trembling every time there's a knock on the door."

"You're not scared, are you?"

"Damn right I am," Marcia said.

"It should help your act," Carella answered and they left.

The administration building for the Naval District that boundaried the city had its offices downtown on Worship Avenue. When Carella and Hawes got back to the squad, Hawes looked up the number in the phone book and dialed it.

"Naval Administration," a voice answered.

"This is the police," Hawes said. "Let me speak to your commanding officer."

"One moment, please." There was a pause and then some clicking on the line.

"Ensign Davis," a voice said.

"Are you the commanding officer?" Hawes asked.

"No, sir. May I help you?"

"This is the police. We're trying to locate a sailor from a—"

"That would fall into the province of the Shore Patrol, sir. One moment, please."

"Look, all I want to—"

The clicking on the line interrupted Hawes.

"Yes, sir?" the operator asked.

"Put this call through to Lieutenant Jergens in Shore Patrol, would you?"

"Yes, sir."

More clicking. Hawes waited.

"Lieutenant Jergens, Shore Patrol," a voice said.

"This is Detective Cotton Hawes," Hawes answered, figuring he'd throw a little rank around among all this brass. "We're looking for an enlisted man named Mickey Carmichael. He's aboard a—"

"What'd he do?" Jergens asked.

"Nothing yet. We want to stop him before—"

"If he didn't do anything, we wouldn't have any record of him. Is he connected with this building?"

"No, he's—"

"Just a moment, I'll get you Personnel."

"I don't want—"

The clicking cut him off again.

"Operator?" Jergens said.

"Yes, sir."

"Put this through to Commander Elliot in Personnel."

"Yes, sir."

Hawes waited.

Click-click.

Click-click.

"Commander Elliot's office," a voice said.

"Is this Commander Elliot?"

"No, sir. This is Chief Yeoman Pickering."

"Let me talk to the commander, Pickering."

"I'm sorry, sir, he's not in right now, sir. Who's calling, please, sir?"

"Let me talk to his superior, will you?" Hawes asked.

"His superior, sir, is commanding officer here, sir. Who's calling please, sir?"

"This is Admiral Hawes!" Hawes shouted. "Connect me with your commanding officer at once!"

"Yes, sir, Admiral. Yes, sir!"

The clicking was frantic now.

"Yes, sir?" the operator asked.

"Put this through to Captain Finchberger," Pickering said. "On the double."

"Yes, sir!"

The clicking clicked again.

"Captain Finchberger's office," a voice said.

"Get me the captain! This is Admiral Hawes!" Hawes said, enjoying himself immensely now.

"Yes, sir!" the voice snapped.

Hawes waited.

The voice that came onto the line wasn't having any damned nonsense.

"Admiral *who*?" it shouted.

"Sir?" Hawes asked, recalling his Navy days and remembering that he was talking to a Naval captain, which is very much different from an Army captain, a Naval captain being a very high rank, indeed, full of scrambled eggs and all sorts of highly polished brass. Considering this, Hawes turned on the oil. "I'm sorry, sir, your secretary must have misunderstood. This is Detective Hawes of the 87th Precinct here in the city. We were wondering if we could have the Navy's assistance on a rather difficult problem."

"What is it, Hawes?" Finchberger said, but he was weakening.

"Sir, we're trying to locate a sailor who was in the city a month ago, and who is perhaps still here. He was off a picket destroyer, sir. His name is—"

"There was a picket destroyer here in June, that's right," Finchberger said. "The USS *Perriwinkle*. She's gone now. Left on the fourth."

"All hands aboard, sir?"

"The commanding officer did not report anyone AOL or AWOL. The ship left with its full complement."

"Have there been any other picket destroyers in port since then, sir?"

"No, there haven't."

"*Any* destroyers at all?"

"We've got one scheduled for the end of the week. Coming up from Norfolk. That's all."

"Would it be the *Perriwinkle*, sir?"

"No, it would not. It would be the *Masterson*."

"Thank you, sir. Then there is no possibility that this sailor is still in the city or scheduled to arrive in the city?"

"Not unless he jumped ship in the middle of the Atlantic," Finchberger said. "The *Perriwinkle* was headed for England."

"Thank you, sir," Hawes said. "You've been very kind."

"Don't pull that admiral routine again, Hawes," Finchberger said, and he hung up.

"Find him?" Carella asked.

Hawes replaced the phone in its cradle.

"He's on his way to Europe," he said.

"That let's him out," Carella said.

"It doesn't let our hooker friend out," Hawes answered.

"No. She might still be the target. I'll call her and tell her not to worry about the sailor. In the meantime, I'll ask Pete for a couple of uniformed men to watch Ida's joint. If she *is* the target, our boy won't try for her with cops around."

"We hope."

Hawes looked up at the white-faced clock on the squadroom wall. It was exactly 11:00 in the morning.

In nine hours, their killer—whoever he was—would strike.

From somewhere across the street in Grover Park, the sun glinted on something shiny, blinking it's rays through the grilled window of the squadroom, flashing momentarily on Hawes's face.

"Draw that shade, will you, Steve?" he asked.

Sam Grossman was a police lieutenant, a laboratory technician, and the man in charge of the police laboratory at Headquarters on High Street, downtown.

Sam was a tall, loosely jointed man who moved with angular nonchalance and ease. He was a gentle man with a craggy face, a man who wore glasses because too much reading as a child had ruined his eyesight. His eyes were blue and mild, guileless eyes that denied the fact that their owner used them to pry into the facts of crime and violence—and very often death. Sam loved lab work, and when he was not busy with his test tubes in an effort to prove the lab's effectiveness in crime detection, he could be found talking to the nearest detective, trying to impress upon him the need for cooperation with the lab.

When the letter from the 87th Precinct had arrived by messenger that morning, Sam had put his men to work on it immediately. The phone call preceding it had urged speed. His men had photographed the letter and sent the photo back to the 87th at once. And then they had begun the task of scrutinizing the letter and the envelope for latent fingerprint impressions before beginning their other tests.

The original letter was handled with the utmost care. Sam sourly reflected that half the cops in the city had probably handled it already, but he had no desire to compound the felony. Carefully, methodically, his men put a very thin, uniform layer of a 10 percent solution of silver nitrate onto the letter, passing the sheet of paper between two rollers that had been moistened with the solution. They waited while the sheet of paper dried, and then they put it under the ultraviolet light. In a few seconds, the prints appeared.

This is what the letter looked like:

There were a lot of fingerprints all over the letter. Sam Grossman had expected as much. The letter had been created by snipping words from newspapers or magazines and pasting them to a sheet of paper. Sam expected that the pasting process would have left finger marks all over the page, and such was exactly the case. Each snip of paper had been pressed to the page so that it would stick. Each word on the page carried its own full complement of prints.

And each print on the page was hopelessly smeared or blurred or overlaid with another print—except for two thumbprints. These thumbprints were on the left-hand side of the page, one close to the top, the other just a little below center. Both were good prints.

Both—unfortunately—belonged to Sergeant Dave Murchison.

Sam sighed. It was a crying shame. He always had to make his point the hard way.

Hawes took the call from Grossman in the interrogation room, where he had gone to study the photo of the letter. The call came at 11:17.

"Hawes?" Grossman said.

"Yes."

"Sam Grossman at the lab. I've got a report on that letter. Since there's a time element on this, I thought I'd give it to you on the phone."

"Shoot," Hawes said.

"Not much help on the prints," Grossman said. "Only two good prints on the letter itself, and they're your desk sergeant's."

"This is the front of the letter?"

"Yes."

"How about the back?"

"Everything smeared. The letter was folded. Whoever folded it ran his bunched fist along the crease. Nothing there, Hawes. I'm sorry."

"And the envelope?"

"Murchison's prints—and yours. Nothing else except some good prints left by a child. Did a child handle the envelope?"

"Yes."

"Well, I've got a good batch of his prints, in case you need them for comparison. Want me to send them over?"

"Please," Hawes said. "What else have you got?"

"On the letter itself, we dug up a few items that might help you. The paste used was five-and-dime stuff put out by a company called Brandy's. They manufacture it in a jar and in a tube. We found a microscopic blue-metallic-paint scraping stuck to one corner of the letter. Their tube is blue, so chances are your letter writer used the tube. That's no help, though. He could have bought the paste anywhere. It's a common item. The paper, though…"

"Yes, what about that?"

"It's a good-rag-content bond, manufactured by the Cartwright Company in Boston, Massachusetts. We checked our watermark file. The catalogue number on the paper is 142Y. It costs about five and a half bucks a ream."

"But it's a Boston company, huh?"

"Yes, but distributed nationally. There's a distributor in this city. Want the name?"

"Please."

"Eastern Shipping. That's on Gage Boulevard in Majesta. Want the phone number?"

"Yes."

"Princeton 4-9800."

Hawes jotted it down. "Anything else?"

"Yes. We know where the letter writer got his words."

"Where?"

"The tip-off was the *T* in the word *tonight*. That *T* is famous, Hawes."

"It's the *New York Times,* isn't it?"

"Exactly. Distributed here, as in every city in the country. I'll confess our newspaper and magazine file doesn't go back too far. But we try to keep abreast of the major dailies and all the big publications. We sometimes get parts of bodies wrapped in newspapers or portions of newspapers. Every once in a while it helps to have a file."

"I see," Hawes said.

"This time we were lucky. Using that *New York Times T* as a springboard, we looked through what we had and pinpointed the sections of the *Times* he used, and the date."

"And they were?"

"He used the magazine section and the book section of the *Times* for Sunday, June twenty-third. We've located enough of the words he's used to eliminate coincidence. For example, *The Lady* came from the book section. Snipped from an ad for the Conrad Richter novel. The word *can* was from an ad in the magazine section for Scandale. That's a woman's undergarment trade name."

"Go ahead."

"The figure eight was obvious, again from the magazine section. An ad for Ballantine beer."

"Anything else?"

"The word *kill* was easy. Not many advertisers use that word unless it's pertinent to their product. This ad said something about killing bathroom odors. 'Kill bathroom odors with—' and the name of the product. In any case, there's no doubt in our minds. He used the June twenty-third *Times.*"

"And this is July twenty-fourth," Hawes said.

"Yeah."

"In other words, he planned this thing as long as a month ago, made up his letter, and then held it until he'd decided on the date for the murder."

"It would seem that way. Unless he used an old paper that was around."

"It would also seem to eliminate a crank."

"It looks legit to me, Hawes," Grossman said. "I was talking to our psychologist upstairs. He didn't seem to think a crank would wait a month between composing a letter and delivering it. He also feels the delivery of the letter was an act of compulsion. He thinks the guy *wants* to be stopped, and he further thinks the letter will give you a clue about *how* to stop him."

"How?" Hawes asked.

"He didn't say."

"Mmmm. Well, have you got anything else for me?"

"That's it. Oh, wait. The guy smokes cigarettes. There were a few grains of tobacco in the envelope. We tested them, but they could have come from any of the major brands."

"Okay, Sam. Thanks a lot."

"Don't mention it. I'll send that kid's prints over. So long."

Grossman hung up. Hawes lifted his copy of the letter from the desk, opened the door, and started for Lieutenant Byrnes's office. It was then that he noticed the chaos in the squadroom.

It was the noise that first attracted him, the sound of shrill voices raised in protest, speculation, and wonder. And then his eyes were assailed with what seemed like an overly patriotic display, a parade for the dead-and-gone Fourth of July. The squadroom was bursting with red, white, and blue. Hawes blinked. Crowding the slatted-rail divider, lined up against the desks and the file cabinets and the windows and the bulletin boards, slouched into every conceivable corner of the room, were at least 8,000 kids in blue dungarees and red-and-white-striped T-shirts.

"Shut up!" Lieutenant Byrnes shouted. "Now, just knock off all this chatter!"

The room modulated slowly into silence.

"Welcome to the Grover Park Nursery School," Carella said to Hawes, smiling.

"Jesus," Hawes said, "we sure as hell have an efficient bunch of patrolmen in this precinct."

The efficient bunch of patrolmen had followed their orders to the letter, rounding up every ten-year-old kid wearing dungarees and a red-striped shirt. They had not asked for birth certificates, and so the kids ranged from seven to thirteen. The T-shirts, too, were not all T-shirts. Some of them sported collars and buttons. But the patrolmen had done their job, and a hasty count of the kids revised Hawes's earlier estimate of 8,000. There were only 7,000. Well, at least three dozen, anyway. Apparently there had been a run on red-striped T-shirts in the neighborhood. Either that, or a new street gang was forming and they had decided upon this as their uniform.

"Which of you kids delivered a letter to this precinct this morning?" Byrnes asked.

"What kinda letter?" one asked.

"What difference does it make? Did you deliver it?"

"Naw," the kid answered.

"Then shut up. Which one of you delivered it?"

Nobody answered.

"Come on, come on, speak up," Byrnes said.

An eight-year-old kid, obviously impressed by the Hollywood effort, piped, "I wanna call my lawyer."

The other kids all laughed.

"Shut up!" Byrnes roared. "Now, listen, you're not in any trouble. We're only trying to locate the man who gave you that letter, that's all. So if you delivered it, speak up."

"What'd he do, this guy?" a twelve-year-old asked.

"Did you deliver the letter?"

"No. I just wanna know what he done, this guy."

"Any of you deliver the letter?" Byrnes asked again. The boys were all shaking their heads. Byrnes turned to Murchison. "How about it, Dave? Recognize one of them?"

"Hard to say," Murchison said. "One thing for sure, he was a blond kid. You can let all the dark-haired kids go. We've got a couple of redheads in there, too. They're no good. This kid was blond."

"Steve, keep only the blonds," Byrnes said, and Carella began walking through the room, tapping boys, telling them to go home. When he'd finished the culling process, the room had thinned down to four blond boys. The other boys idled on the other side of the slatted-rail divider, watching.

"Beat it," Hawes said. "Go home."

The boys left reluctantly.

Of the four blonds remaining, two were at least twelve years old.

"They're too old," Murchison said.

"You two can go," Byrnes told them, and the boys drifted out. Byrnes turned to one of the remaining two.

"How old are you, sonny?" he asked.

"Eight."

"What do you say, Dave?"

"He's not the kid."

"How about the other one?"

"Him neither."

"Well, that's—" Byrnes seemed suddenly stabbed with pain. "Hawes, stop those other kids before they get past the desk. Get their names, for Christ's sake. We'll put them on the radio. Otherwise we'll be getting the same damn kids in here all day long. Hurry up!"

Hawes went through the railing and sprinted for the steps. He stopped some of the kids in the muster room, rounded up the rest on the sidewalk and sent them all back into the precinct. One kid sighed reluctantly and patted a huge German shepherd on the head.

"You wait, Prince," he said. "I gotta handle this again," and then he walked into the building.

Hawes looked at the dog. The idea clicked into his mind. He ran into the building, climbed the steps, and rushed into the squadroom.

"A dog!" he said. "Suppose it's a dog!"

"Huh?" Byrnes asked. "Did you stop those kids?"

"Yes, but it could be a dog!"

"*What* could be a dog?"

"Lady! The Lady!"

Carella spoke instantly. "He could be right, Pete. How many dogs named Lady do you suppose there are in the precinct?"

"I don't know," Byrnes said. "You think the nut who wrote that letter…?"

"It's a possibility."

"All right, get on the phone. Meyer! Meyer!"

"Yah, Pete?"

"Start taking these kids' names. Jesus, this place is turning into a madhouse!"

Turning, Byrnes stamped into his office.

Carella's call to the Bureau of Licenses revealed that there were thirty-one licensed dogs named Lady within the precinct territory. God alone knew how many unlicensed dogs of the same name there were.

He reported his information to Byrnes.

Byrnes told him that if a man wanted to kill a goddamn lady dog, that was his business and Byrnes wasn't going to upset his whole damn squad tracking down every bitch in the precinct.

They'd find out about it the minute the dog was killed, anyway, and then they might or might not try to find the canine killer.

He suggested that in the meantime Hawes call Eastern Shipping in an attempt to find out whether or not any shops in the precinct carried the paper the letter was pasted on.

"And close the goddamn door!" he shouted as Carella left.

It was 11:32 A.M.

The sun was climbing steadily into the sky and now was almost at its zenith, its rays baking the asphalt and the concrete, sending shimmering waves of heat up from the pavements.

There was no breeze in the park.

The man with the binoculars sat atop a high outcropping of rock, but it was no cooler there than it was on the paths that wound through the park. The man wore blue-gabardine trousers and a cotton-mesh short-sleeved sports shirt. He sat in cross-legged Indian fashion, his elbows resting on his knees, the binoculars trained on the police precinct across the street.

There was an amused smile on the man's face.

He watched the kids streaming out of the police station, and the smile widened. His letter was bringing results. His letter had set the precinct machinery in motion, and he watched the results of that motion now, and there was a strange pulsing excitement within him as he wondered if he would be caught.

They won't catch me, he thought.

But maybe they will.

The excitement within him was contradictory. He wanted to elude them, but at the same time he relished the idea of a chase, a desperate gun battle, the culminating scene of a carefully planned murder. Tonight he would kill. Yes. There was no backing away from that. Yes. He had to kill, he knew that, there was no other way, that was it, yes. Tonight. They could not stop him, but maybe they would. They could not stop him.

A man was leaving the precinct, coming down the stone steps.

He focused the binoculars tightly on the man's face. A detective, surely. On business his letter had provoked? His grin widened.

The detective had red hair. The hair caught the rays of the brilliant sun. There was a white streak over one temple. He followed the detective with his binoculars. The detective got into an automobile, an unmarked police car, undoubtedly. The car pulled away from the curb quickly.

They're in a hurry, the man thought, lowering the binoculars. He looked at his wristwatch.

11:35.

They haven't got much time, he thought. *They haven't got much time to stop me.*

The bookshop was unusual for the 87th Precinct neighborhood. You did not expect to find a store selling books in such a neighborhood. You expected all the reading matter to be in drugstore racks, and you expected sadistic mysteries like *I, the Hangman*, historical novels like *See My Bosom*, dramas of the Old West like *Sagebrush Sixgun*.

The shop was called Books, Incorporated. It huddled in one of the side streets between two tenements, below street level. You passed through an old iron gate, walked down five steps, and were face to face with the plateglass window of the shop and its display of books. A sign in the window said, "We Stock Spanish-language books." Another sign said, "*Aquí habla Español.*"

In the right-hand corner of the window, lettered onto the glass in gold gilt, were the words CHRISTINE MAXWELL, PROP.

Hawes walked down the steps and opened the screen door of the shop. A bell over the door tinkled. The shop instantly touched something deep in his memory. He felt he had been here before, had seen the dusty racks and shelves, had sniffed of the musty bookbindings, the intimate smell of stored knowledge. Had he browsed in such a shop on a rainy day in the side streets fringing The Quarter downtown? Was this *The Haunted Bookshop* come to life, a stationary "Parnassus on Wheels"? He remembered the Morley books from his youth, and he wished he had time to browse, wished that time were not so important right now. There was a friendliness and warmth to the shop, and he wanted to soak it up, sponge it into his bones, and he wished his visit were not such an urgent one, wished he had come for information that had nothing to do with sudden death.

"Yes?" the voice said.

He broke off his thoughts abruptly. The voice was gentle, a voice that belonged in the shop. He turned.

The girl stood before the shelves of brown-backed books, stood in an almost mist-like radiance, fragile, tender, gentle, against the musty cracked brown. Her hair was blonde, whisper-like tendrils softly cradling the oval of her face. Her eyes were blue and wide, the soft blue of a spring sky, the delicate blue of a lilac. There was a tentative smile on her full mouth, a mouth kissed by the seasons. And because she was a human being, and because it was a hot day in July, there was a thin film of perspiration on her upper lip. And because she was a human being and not a memory and not a dream and not a maiden from some legendary Camelot, Hawes fell in love with her instantly.

"Hello," he said. There was surprise in his voice, but it was not a wise guy's "Hell-*lo!*" It was more an awed whisper, and the girl looked at him and again said, "Yes?"

"Perhaps you can help me," Hawes said, reflecting on the fact that he fell in and out of love too easily, musing upon the theory that all true love was love at first sight, in which case he had been truly in love a great many times, but nonetheless studying the girl and thinking, *I love her, so the hell with you.*

"Were you looking for a book, sir?" the girl asked

"Are you Miss Maxwell?" he asked.

"*Mrs.* Maxwell," she corrected.

"Oh," he said. "Oh."

"Was there a book you wanted?"

He looked at her left hand. She was not wearing a wedding band. "I'm from the police," he said. "Detective Hawes, 87th Squad."

"Is something wrong?"

"No. I'm trying to track down a piece of stationery. Eastern Shipping says you're the only store in the precinct that carries the paper."

"Which paper is that?" Christine asked.

"Cartwright 142Y."

"Oh, yes," she said.

"Do you carry it?"

"Yes?" She made it a question.

"Run this shop with your husband, do you?" Hawes asked.

"My husband is dead," she said. "He was a Navy pilot He was killed in the Battle of the Coral Sea."

"I'm sorry," Hawes said genuinely.

"Please don't," she said. "It's been a long time. A person can't live in the past, you know." She smiled gently.

"You don't look that old," he said. "I mean, to have been married during World War Two."

"I got married when I was seventeen," she said.

"Which makes you?"

"Thirty-three," she said.

"You look much younger."

"Thank you."

"I'd say you were barely twenty-one."

"Thank you, but I'm not. Really."

They looked at each other silently for a moment.

"It seems strange," Hawes said. "To find a shop like this. In this neighborhood, I mean."

"I know. That's why it's here."

"What do you mean?"

"Well, there's enough deprivation in this neighborhood. It needn't extend to books."

"Do you get a lot of people coming in?" Hawes asked.

"More now than in the beginning. Actually, the stationery supplies are what keep the shop going. But it's better now than it was. You'd be surprised how many people want to read good books."

"Are you afraid of the neighborhood?"

"Should I be?" she asked.

"Well…a pretty girl like you. I mean, this isn't the best neighborhood in the world."

The girl seemed surprised. "The people here are poor," she said. "But *poor* isn't necessarily synonymous with *dangerous*."

"That's true," he said.

"People are people. The people who live here are no better, no worse, than the people who live in swanky Stewart City."

"Where do you live, Miss—*Mrs.* Maxwell?"

"In Isola."

"Where?"

"Why do you want to know?"

"I'd like to see you sometime," Hawes said.

Christine was silent for a moment. She looked at Hawes penetratingly, as if she were trying to read his mind and his motives. Then she said, "All right. When?"

"Tonight?" he asked.

"All right."

"Wait a minute," he said. He thought for a moment. "Well, it'll be over by eight o'clock either way," he said. "Yes, tonight is fine."

"What'll be over by eight?"

"A case we're working on."

"How do you know it'll be over by eight? Do you have a crystal ball?"

Hawes smiled. "I'll tell you about it tonight. May I pick you up at nine? Is that too late for you?"

"Tomorrow's a working day," she said.

"I know. I thought we'd have a drink and talk a little."

"All right," she said.

"Where?" he asked.

"711 40th Boulevard. Do you know where that is?"

"I'll find it. That's lucky. Seven-eleven."

Christine smiled. "Shall I dress?"

"We'll find a quiet cocktail lounge," he said. "If that's all right with you."

"Yes, that's fine. Air-conditioned, please."

"What else?" he said, spreading his hands.

"Are you sensitive about the white streak in your hair?"

"Not at all."

"If you are, I won't ask."

"You can ask. I got knifed once. It grew back this way. A puzzle for medical science to unravel."

"Knifed? By a person, do you mean?"

"Sure," he said.

"Oh." It was a very tiny "Oh."

Hawes looked at her. "People do…Well, people do get knifed, you know."

"Yes, of course. I imagine a detective…" She stopped. "What was it you wanted to know about the stationery?"

"Well, how much of it do you stock?"

"All my paper supplies come from Cartwright. The 142Y comes in reams and also in smaller packages of a hundred sheets."

"Do you sell a lot of it?"

"Of the smaller packages, yes. The reams move more slowly."

"How many smaller packs have you sold in the past month?"

"Oh, I couldn't possibly say. A lot."

"And the reams?"

"The reams are easier to check. I got six reams at the beginning of June. I can count how many are left."

"Would you, please?" he asked.

"Certainly."

She walked to the back of the shop. Hawes pulled a book from the shelf and began leafing through it. When Christine returned, she said, "That's one of my favorites. Have you read it?"

"Yes. A long time ago."

"I read it when I was still a girl." She smiled briefly, put the book out of her mind, and said, "I have two reams left. I'm glad you stopped in. I'll have to reorder."

"That means you sold four, correct?"

"Yes."

"Would you remember to whom?"

"I know to whom I sold two of them. The others I couldn't say."

"Who?" Hawes asked.

"A young man who comes in here regularly for 142Y. He buys at least a ream a month. He's one of the chief reasons I keep it in stock."

"Do you know his name?"

"Yes. Philip Bannister."

"Does he live in the neighborhood?"

"I imagine so. Whenever he's come into the shop, he's been dressed casually. He came in once wearing Bermuda shorts."

"Bermuda shorts?" Hawes asked, astonished. "In _this_ neighborhood?"

"People are people," the girl reminded him.

"You don't know where he lives, though?" Hawes said.

"No. It must be close by, though."

"What makes you say that?"

"He's often come in with shopping in his arms. Groceries, you know. I'm sure he lives close by."

"I'll check it," Hawes said. "And I'll see you tonight at nine."

"At nine," Christine said. She paused. "I'm…I'm looking forward to seeing you again," she said.

"So am I," he answered.

"Good-bye," she said.

"Good-bye."

The bell over the door tinkled when he left.

The telephone directory listed a Philip Bannister at 1592 South 10th. Hawes called the squad to let Carella know where he was going, and then he drove to Bannister's place.

South Tenth was a typical precinct street, crowded with tenements and humanity, overlooked by fire escapes cluttered with the paraphernalia of life. The fire escapes were loaded today. Today every woman in the neighborhood had said to hell with cleaning the house. Today every woman in the neighborhood had put on her lightest clothing and stepped out onto the fire escape in the hope of catching any breeze that might rustle through the concrete canyon. Radios had been plugged into extension cords that trailed back into the apartments, and music flooded the street. Pitchers of lemonade, cans of beer beaded with cold sweat, milk bottles full of ice water, rested on the fire escapes. The women sat and drank and fanned themselves, their skirts pulled up over their knees, some of them sitting in shorts and halters, some of them sitting in slips, all of them trying desperately to beat the heat.

Hawes pulled the car to the curb, cut the engine, mopped his brow, and stepped from his small oven into the larger oven that was the street. He was wearing lightweight trousers and a cotton sports shirt open at the throat, but he was sweating nonetheless. He thought suddenly of Fats Donner and the Turkish bath, and felt immediately cooler.

1592 was a dowdy gray tenement set between two similarly dowdy and similarly gray tenements. Hawes climbed the front stoop, walking past two young girls who were discussing Eddie Fisher. One of them couldn't understand what he'd seen in Debbie Reynolds. She herself was built better than Debbie Reynolds, and she was sure Eddie had noticed her that time she'd got his autograph outside the stage door. Hawes went into the building, wishing he could sing.

A small neatly lettered white card told him that Philip Bannister lived in Apartment 21. Hawes wiped sweat from his lip and then climbed to the second floor. Every door on the floor was open in an attempt to produce a cross-current circulation of air. The attempt failed miserably. Not a breeze stirred in the hallway. The door to Apartment 21 was open, too. From somewhere inside

the apartment, Hawes heard the unmistakable chatter of a typewriter. He knocked on the doorjamb.

"Anybody home?" he called.

The typewriter continued its incessant jabbering.

"Hey! Anybody home?"

The clatter of the keys stopped abruptly. "Who is it?" a voice
shouted.

"Police," Hawes said.

"*Who?*" The voice was utterly incredulous.

"Police."

"Just a second."

Hawes heard the typewriter start up again. It went furiously
for some three and a half minutes and then stopped. He heard
a chair being scraped back, heard the pad of bare feet through
the apartment. A thin man in undershirt and striped undershorts
came into the kitchen and walked to the front door. He cocked his
head to one side, his bright brown eyes gleaming.

"Did you say *police?*" he asked.

"Yes, I did."

"It can't be Grandfather because he's dead. I know Dad drinks
a bit, but what kind of trouble can he be in?"

Hawes smiled. "I'd like to ask you a few questions. That is, if
you're Philip Bannister."

"The very same. And you are?"

"Detective Hawes, 87th Squad."

"A real cop," Bannister said appreciatively. "A real live detective. Well, well, enter. What's the matter? Am I typing too loud?
Did that bitch complain about it?"

"What bitch?"

"My landlady. Come in, make yourself homely. She's threatened to call the cops if I type at night again. Is that what this is?"

"No," Hawes said.

"Sit down," Bannister said, indicating one of the chairs at the kitchen table. "Want a cold beer?"

"I can use one."

"So can I. When do you think we'll get some rain?"

"I couldn't say."

"Neither could I. Neither can the Weather Bureau. I think they get their forecasts by reading yesterday's forecast in the newspapers." Bannister opened the icebox door and pulled out two cans of beer. "Ice melts like hell in this weather. You mind drinking it from the can?"

"Not at all."

He punctured both cans and handed one to Hawes.

"To the noble and the pure," he toasted, and he drank. Hawes drank with him. "Ahhhhh, good," Bannister said. "The simple pleasures. Nothing like them. Who needs money?"

"You live here alone, Bannister?" Hawes asked.

"Entirely alone. Except when I have visitors, which is rarely. I enjoy women, but I can't afford them."

"You employed?"

"Sort of. I'm a freelance writer."

"Magazines?"

"I am currently working on a book," Bannister said.

"Who's your publisher?"

"I have no publisher. I wouldn't be living in this rat trap if I had a publisher. I'd be lighting cigars with twenty-dollar bills, and I'd be dating all the high-class fashion models in the city."

"Is that what successful writers do?"

"That's what this writer is going to do when he's successful."

"Did you buy a ream of Cartwright 142Y recently?" Hawes asked.

"Huh?"

"Cartwright 14   "

"Yeah," Bannister said. "How the hell did you know that?"

"Do you know a prostitute called The Lady?"

"Huh?"

"Do you know a prostitute called The Lady?" Hawes repeated.

"No. What? What did you say?"

"I said—"

"Are you kidding?"

"I'm serious."

"A prost—hell, no!" Bannister seemed to get suddenly indignant. "How would I know a prost? Are you kidding?"

"Do you know *anyone* called 'The Lady'?"

"The Lady? What is this?"

"The Lady. Think."

"I don't have to think. I don't know anybody called The Lady. What is this?"

"May I see your desk?"

"I don't have a desk. Listen, the joke has gone far enough. I don't know how you found out what kind of typing paper I use, and I don't particularly care. All I know is that you're sitting there drinking my good beer, which costs me money Dad works hard to earn, and asking me foolish questions about prost...Now, what is this, huh? What is this?"

"May I see your desk, please?"

"I don't have a goddamn desk! I work on a table!"

"May I see that?"

"All right, all right, be mysterious!" Bannister shouted. "Be a big-shot mysterious detective. Go ahead. Be my guest. The table's in the other room. Don't mess up anything, or I'll call the goddamn commissioner."

Hawes went into the other room. A typewriter was on the table, together with a pile of typed sheets, a package of carbon paper, and an opened box of typing paper.

"Do you have any paste?" Hawes asked.

"Of course not. What would I be doing with paste?"

"What are your plans for tonight, Bannister?"

"Who wants to know?" Bannister asked, pulling back his shoulders dignifiedly, looking the way Napoleon must have looked in his underwear.

"I do," Hawes said.

"Suppose I don't care to answer you?"

Hawes shrugged. The shrug was very meaningful. Bannister studied the shrug and then said, "Okay. I'm going to the ballet with Mother."

"Where?"

"The City Theater."

"What time?"

"It starts at eight-thirty."

"Your mother live here in the city?"

"No. She lives out on Sand's Spit. The East Shore."

"Is she well fixed, would you say?"

"I would say so, yes."

"Would you call her a suburban lady?"

"I would," Bannister admitted.

"A lady?"

"Yes."

Hawes hesitated. "Do you get along with her?"

"With Mother? Of course I do."

"How does she feel about your writing?"

"She feels I have great talent."

"Does she like the idea of your living in a slum neighborhood?"

"She would rather I lived home, but she respects my wishes."

"The family's supporting you, is that right?"

"That's right."

"How much?'

"Sixty-five a week."

"Mother ever oppose this?"

"The money, you mean? No. Why should she? I spent much more than that when I was living at home."

"Who paid for the ballet tickets tonight?"

"Mother."

"Where were you this morning at about eight o'clock, Bannister?"

"Right here."

"Anybody with you?"

"No."

"Anybody see you here?"

"The typewriter was going," Bannister said. "Ask any of my neighbors. Unless they're all dead, they heard it. Why? What am I supposed to have done at eight o'clock this morning?"

"What paper do you read on Sundays?" Hawes asked.

"The *Graphic*."

"Any out-of-town papers?"

"Like what?"

"Like the *New York Times*?"

"Yes. I buy the *Times*."

"Every Sunday?"

"Yes. I like to see what pap is on the best-seller list each week."

"Do you know where the station house is?"

"The police station, you mean?"

"Yes."

"It's near the park, isn't it?"

"Is it, or isn't it?" Hawes asked.

"Yes, it is. I still don't understand—"

"What time are you meeting your mother?"

"Eight," Bannister said.

"Eight tonight. Do you own a gun?"

"No."

"Any other weapon?"

"No."

"Have you had any arguments with your mother recently?"

"No."

"With any other woman?"

"No."

"What do you call your mother?"

"Mother."

"Anything else."

"Mom."

"Any nicknames?"

"Sometimes I call her Carol. That's her name."

"Ever call her The Lady?"

"No. Are we back to that again?"

"Ever call *anybody* The Lady?"

"No."

"What do you call your landlady, the bitch who said she'd call the cops if you typed at night?"

"I call her Mrs. Nelson. I also call her 'The Bitch.'"

"Has she given you a lot of trouble?"

"Only about the typing."

"Do you like her?"

"Not particularly."

"Do you hate her?"

"No. I hardly ever think about her, to tell the truth."

"Bannister…"

"Yes?"

"A detective will probably follow you to the ballet tonight. He'll be with you when—"

"What do you mean? What am I supposed to have done?"

"—when you leave this apartment, and when you meet your mother, and when you take your seat. I'm telling you this in case—"

"What the hell is this, a police state?"

"—in case you had any rash ideas. Do you understand me, Bannister?"

"No, I don't. The rashest idea I have is buying Mother an ice cream soda after the show."

"Good, Bannister. Keep it that way."

"Cops," Bannister said. "If you're finished, I'd like to get back to work."

"I'm finished," Hawes said. "Thank you for your time. And remember. There'll be a cop with you."

"Balls," Bannister said, and he sat at his table and began typing.

Hawes left the apartment. He checked with the three other tenants on the floor, two of whom were willing to swear (like drunken sailors!) that Bannister's damn machine had been going at 8:00 that morning. In fact, it had started going at 6:30, and hadn't stopped since.

Hawes thanked them and went back to the squad.

It was 12:23.

Hawes was hungry.

Meyer Meyer had raised the shade covering the grilled window facing the park, so that sunshine splashed onto the desk near the window where the men were having lunch.

From where Carella sat at the end of the desk facing the window and the park, he could see out across the street, could see the greenery rolling away from the stone wall that divided the park from the pavement.

"Suppose this isn't a specific lady?" Meyer asked. "Suppose we're on the wrong track?"

"What do you mean?" Carella asked, biting into a sandwich. The sandwich had been ordered at Charlie's Delicatessen, around the corner. It nowhere compared with the sandwiches Carella's wife, Teddy, made.

"We're assuming this nut has a particular dame on his mind," Meyer said. "A dame called The Lady. This may not be so."

"Go ahead," Hawes said.

"This is a terrible sandwich," Carella said.

"They get worse all the time," Meyer agreed. "There's a new place, Steve. The Golden Pot. Did you see it? It's on Fifth, just off Culver Avenue. Willis ate there. Says it's pretty good."

"Does he deliver?" Carella asked.

"If he doesn't, he's passing up a gold mine," Meyer said. "With all the *fressers* in this precinct."

"What about The Lady?" Hawes asked.

"On my lunch hour he wants me to think, yet," Meyer said.

"Do we need that shade up?" Carella asked.

"Why not?" Meyer said. "Let the sunshine in."

"Something's blinking in my eyes," Carella said.

"So move your chair."

Carella shoved back his chair.

"What about—" Hawes started.

"All right, all right," Meyer said. "This one is eager. He's bucking for commissioner."

"He's liable to make it," Carella said.

"Suppose you were pasting up this damn letter?" Meyer asked. "Suppose you were looking through the *New York Times* for words? Suppose all you wanted to say was, 'I'm going to kill a woman tonight at eight. Try and stop me.' Do you follow me so far?"

"I follow you," Hawes said.

"Okay. You start looking. You can't find the word *eight*, so you improvise. You cut out a Ballantine beer thing, and you use that for the figure eight. You can't find the words *I'm going*, but you do find *I will*, so you use those instead. Okay, why can't the same thing apply to The Lady?"

"What do you mean?"

"You want to say *a woman*. You search through the damn paper, and you can't find those words. You're looking through the book section, and you spot the ad for the Conrad Richter novel. 'Why not?' you say to yourself. Woman, lady, the same thing. So you cut out *The Lady*. It happens to be capitalized because it's the title of a novel. That doesn't bother you because it conveys the meaning you want. But it can set the cops off on a wild-goose chase looking for a capitalized Lady when she doesn't really exist."

"If this guy had the patience to cut out and paste up every letter in the word *tonight*," Carella said, "then he knew exactly what he wanted to say, and if he couldn't find the exact word, he created it."

"Maybe, maybe not," Hawes said.

"There are only so many ways to say *tonight*," Meyer said.

"He could have said *this evening*," Carella said. "I mean, using your theory. But he wanted to say *tonight*, so he clipped out every letter he needed to form the word. I don't buy your theory, Meyer." He moved his chair again. "That damn thing is still blinking in the park."

"Okay, don't buy it," Meyer said. "I'm just saying this nut may be ready to kill *any* woman, and not a *specific* woman called 'The Lady.'"

Carella was pensive.

"If that's the case," Hawes said, "we've got nothing to go on. The victim could be any woman in the city. Where do we start?"

"I don't know," Meyer said. He shrugged and sipped at his coffee. "I don't know."

"In the Army," Carella said slowly, "we were always warned about…"

Meyer turned to him. "Huh?" he asked.

"Binoculars," Carella said. "Those are binoculars."

"What do you mean?"

"In the park," he said. "The blinking. Somebody's using binoculars."

"Okay," Meyer said, shrugging it off. "But if the victim *is* any woman, we've got about a chance in five million of stopping—"

"Who'd be training binoculars on the precinct?" Hawes asked slowly.

The men fell suddenly silent.

"Can he see into this room?" Hawes asked.

"Probably," Carella said. Unconsciously, their voices had dropped to whispers, as if their unseen observer could also hear them.

"Just keep sitting and talking," Hawes whispered. "I'll go out and down the back way."

"I'll go with you," Carella said.

"No. He may run if he sees too many of us leaving."

"Do you think...?" Meyer started.

"I don't know," Hawes said, rising slowly.

"You can save us a lot of time," Carella whispered. "Good luck, Cotton."

Hawes emerged into the alley that ran behind the precinct just outside the detention cells on the ground floor. He slammed the heavy steel door shut behind him, and then started through the alley. Idiotically, his heart was pounding.

Easy does it, he told himself. We've got to play this easy or the bird will fly, and we'll be left with The Lady again, or maybe Anywoman, Anywoman in a city teeming with women of all shapes and sizes. So, easy. Play it easy. Sprinkle the salt onto the bird's tail, and if the bastard tries to run, clobber him or shoot him, but play it easy, slow and easy, play it like a *Dragnet* copy, with all the time in the world, about to interrogate the slowest talker in the United States.

He ran to the alley mouth and then cut into the street. The sidewalk was packed with people sucking in fetid air. A stickball game was in progress up the street, and farther down toward the end of the block, a bunch of kids had turned on a fire hydrant and were romping in the released lunge of water, many of them fully clothed. Some of the kids, Hawes noticed, were wearing dungarees and striped T-shirts. He turned right, putting the stickball game and the fire hydrant behind him. What does a good cop do on the hottest day of the year? he wondered. Allow the kids to waste the city's water supply and cause possible danger should the fire department need that hydrant? Or use a Stillson wrench on the hydrant and force the kids back into a sweltering, hot inactivity, an inactivity that causes street gangs and street rumbles and possibly more danger than a fire would cause?

What does the good cop do? Side with the madam of a whorehouse or side with the good citizen trying to cheat her?

Why should cops have to worry about philosophy, Hawes wondered, worrying about philosophy all the while.

He was running.

He was running, and he was sweating like a basement coldwater pipe—but the park was dead ahead, and the man with he binoculars was in that park somewhere.

"Is he still there?" Meyer asked.

"Yes," Carella said.

"Jesus, I'm afraid to move. Do you think he tipped to Hawes?"

"I don't think so."

"One good thing," Meyer said.

"What's that?"

"With all this action, my sandwich tastes better."

The man in the park sat cross-legged on the huge rock, the binoculars pointed at the precinct. There were two cops seated at the desk now, eating sandwiches and talking. The big redheaded one had got up a few minutes ago and leisurely walked away from the desk. Perhaps he'd gone for a glass of water or maybe a cup of coffee? Did they make coffee inside a precinct? Were they allowed to do that? In any case, he had not come out of the building, so he was still inside somewhere.

Maybe he'd been called by the captain or the lieutenant or whoever was his superior. Maybe the captain was all in a dither about the letter and wanted action instead of men sitting around having lunch.

In a way, their having lunch annoyed him. He knew they had to eat, of course—*everybody* has to eat, even cops—but hadn't they taken his letter seriously? Didn't they know he was going to kill? Wasn't it their job to stop someone from killing? For Christ's sake, hadn't he warned them? Hadn't he given them every possible chance to stop him? So why the hell were they sitting around eating sandwiches and chatting? Was this what the city paid cops for?

Disgustedly, he put down the binoculars.

He wiped sweat from his upper lip. His lip felt funny, swollen. Cursing the heat, he pulled a handkerchief from his back pocket.

"It's gone," Carella said.

"What! What!"

"The blinking. It's gone."

"Can Hawes be there already?" Meyer asked.

"No, it's too soon. Maybe the guy's leaving. Goddammit, why didn't we—"

"There it is! The blinking, Steve. He's still there!"

Carella sighed heavily. His hands were clenched on the desktop. He forced himself to pick up his coffee container and sip it. *Come on, Cotton*, he thought. *Move!*

He ran along the park's paths, wondering where the man with the binoculars was. People turned to look at him as he hurried by. It was strange to see a man running at any time, but especially strange on a day as hot as this one. Invariably the passersby looked behind Hawes to see who was chasing him, fully expecting a uniformed cop with a drawn gun in hot pursuit.

A high spot, he figured. If he's able to see the second floor of the precinct, it had to be from a high spot. The brow of a hill or a big rock, but something high, something close to the street where the park ground slopes up to meet the pavement.

Is he armed?

If he's going to kill someone tonight, he's probably armed right now, too. Unconsciously, Hawes touched his back hip pocket, felt the reassuring bulge of his .38. Should he take the gun out now? No. Too many people on the paths. A gun might panic them. One of them might think Hawes was on the opposite side of the law and get heroic, try to stop an escaping thief. No. The gun stayed where it was for now.

He began climbing into the bushes, feeling the slope of the ground beneath his feet. Somewhere high, he thought. It has to be high, or the man can't see. The ground was sharply sloping now, gently rolling grass and earth giving way to a steeply pitched outcropping of rock. Is this the rock? Hawes wondered. Is this the right rock? Is my bird up here?

He drew his .38.

He was breathing hard from the climb. Sweat stained his armpits and the back of his shirt. Small pebbles had found their way into his shoes.

He reached the top of the rock. There was no one there.

In the distance, he could see the precinct. And off to the left, sitting on another high rock, he could see a man crouched over a pair of binoculars. Hawes's heart unexpectedly lurched into his throat.

"What do you see?" Meyer asked.

"Nothing."

"He's still there?"

"The sun's still on the binoculars."

"Where the hell is Hawes!"

"It's a big park," Carella said charitably.

Sitting on the rock, the man with the binoculars thought he heard a sound in the bushes. Slowly he turned, lowering the glasses. Barely breathing, he listened.

He could feel the hackles at the back of his neck rising. Suddenly, he was drenched with sweat. He wiped beads of perspiration from the swollen feel of his upper lip.

There was an unmistakable thrashing in the woods.

He listened.

Was it a kid?

Lovers?

Or a cop?

Run, his mind shrieked. The thought ricocheted inside his skull, but he sat riveted to the rock. They'll stop me, he thought.

But so soon? So soon? After all the planning? To be stopped so soon?

The noise in the woods was closer now. He saw the glint of sunlight on metal. Goddammit, why hadn't he taken the gun with him? Why hadn't he prepared for something like this? His eyes anxiously scanned the barren surface of the rock. There was a high bush at the base of the stone surface. Crawling on his belly, the binoculars clutched in his right hand, he moved toward the bush. The sunlight caught at something bright, something nonmetallic this time. Red. Red hair! The cop who'd left the desk! He held his breath. The thrashing in the woods stopped. From where he crouched behind the bush, he could see the red hair and only that. And then the head ducked and then reappeared. The cop was advancing. He would pass directly in front of the bush.

The man with the binoculars waited. His hand on the metal was sweating. He could see the cop plainly now, advancing slowly, a gun in his right hand.

Patiently, he waited. Maybe he wouldn't be seen. Maybe if he stayed right where he was, he wouldn't be discovered. No. No, that was foolish. He had to get out of this. He had to get out of it or be caught, and it was too soon to be caught, too damned soon.

Hefting the binoculars like a mace, he waited.

From where Hawes advanced through the bushes, he could hear no sound. The park seemed to have gone suddenly still. The birds were no longer chattering in the trees. The sound of muted voices, which hung on the air like a swarm of insects, drifting over the paths and the lake and the trees, had suddenly quieted. There was only the bright sun overhead and the beginnings of the sloping rock, a huge bush on Hawes's left, and the frightening sudden silence.

He could feel danger, could sense it in every nerve ending, could feel it throbbing in every bone marrow. He had felt this way the time he'd been knifed, could remember the startling appearance of the blade, the naked lightbulb glinting on metal, the hurried, desperate lunge for his back pocket and his revolver. He could remember the blurred swipe of the blade, the sudden warmth over his left temple, the feel of blood gushing onto his face. And then, unable to reach his gun before the slashing knife was pulled back, he had struck out with his fists, struck repeatedly until the knife had clattered to the hallway floor, until his assailant had been a blubbering quivering hulk against the wall, and still he had hit him, hit him until his knuckles had bled.

This time he had a gun in his hand. This time he was ready. And still, danger prickled his scalp, rushed up his spinal column with tingling ferocity.

Cautiously, he advanced.

The blow struck him on his right wrist.

The blow was sharp, the biting impact of metal hitting bone. His hand opened, and the .38 clattered to the rock surface. He whirled in time to see the man raise the binoculars high. He brought his hands up to protect his face. The binoculars descended, the lenses catching sunlight, glittering crazily. For a maniacal, soundless moment he saw the man's frenzied, twisted face, and then the binoculars struck, smashing into Hawes's hands. He felt intense pain. He clenched his fists, threw a punch, and then saw the binoculars go up again and down, and he knew they would strike his face this time. Blindly, he clutched at them.

He felt metal strike his palms, and then he closed his hands and wrenched at the glasses with all his strength, pulling at them. He felt them come free. The man stood stock-still for just a moment, surprise stamped on his face. Then he broke into a run.

Hawes dropped the glasses.

The man was in the bushes by the time Hawes retrieved the .38.

He picked up the gun and fired into the air. He fired into the air again, and then he thrashed into the bushes after the man.

When Carella heard the shots in the squadroom, he shoved back his chair and said, "Let's go, Meyer."

They found Hawes sitting on a patch of grass in the park. He'd lost their man, he said. They examined his wrist and his hands. There didn't seem to be any broken bones. He led them back to the rock where he'd been ambushed, and again, he said, "I lost him. I lost the bastard."

"Maybe you didn't," Carella said.

Spreading a handkerchief over his palm, he picked up the binoculars.

At the police lab, Sam Grossman identified the glasses as having been made by a firm named Pieter-Vondiger. The serial number told him the glasses had been manufactured sometime during 1952. The air-glass surfaces were not antireflection coated, and so the binoculars had not been made for the Armed Forces, as many of the firm's glasses had been during that time. A call to the company assured Sam that the model was no longer being sold in retail stores, having been replaced by more recent, improved models. Nonetheless, he prepared a chart on the glasses for the cops of the 87th, while his men went over the glasses for fingerprints. Sam Grossman was a methodical man, and it was his contention that the smallest, most insignificant-seeming piece of information might prove valuable to the men investigating a case. And so he wrote down every particular of the field glasses.

Magnification: 8 diameters   Exit pupil: 3.5 mm.
Objective lenses: 30 mm.   Relative brightness: 12.3
   diameter   Field at 1,000 yards: 135
Angular field: 7° 44'   yds.
Pupilary distance: 48 to 72   Length closed: 4 ¼"
   am.   Length extended: 4⅝"
    Weight: 18 oz.

The glasses were central focusing, right ocular adjustable individually. The price of the glasses when new, sold together with a stiff-sole leather casing and straps, was $92.50.

There were two sets of prints on the glasses. One belonged to Cotton Hawes. The other, which—because of the very way in which binoculars must be held—consisted of fairly good thumb and finger impressions for both hands, had been left on the glasses by Hawes's assailant. Photos were taken of the prints. One photo was sent immediately to the Bureau of Criminal Identification. The other was photo-transmitted to the Federal Bureau of Investigation in Washington. Each agency was asked for extreme speed in making a possible identification from the prints.

Sam Grossman prayed that the man who'd left the prints on the glasses had also left a record of those prints somewhere in the United States.

It was 1:10 P.M.

Lieutenant Byrnes spread the newspaper on his desk. "How about this, Hawes?" he asked.

Hawes looked at the page, his eye running down it until he found the ad. The ad said:

Appearing now at the Brisson Roof!
Jay "Lady" Astor

Piano stylings and Songs
in the
Lady Astor manner

There was a picture of a dark-haired girl in a skintight evening dress, smiling.

"I didn't know she was in the city," Hawes said.

"Ever hear of her?"

"Yes. She's pretty popular. Sophisticated stuff, you know. Cole Porter, like that. And lots of special material with off-color lyrics in impeccable taste."

"How's your wrist?"

"Fine," Hawes said, feeling it with his left hand.

"Do you want to look her up?"

"Sure," Hawes said.

The phone on Byrnes's desk rang. He picked it up.

"Byrnes here," he said. He listened. "Sure, put him on, Dave." He covered the mouthpiece. "The lab," he said to Hawes. He uncovered the mouthpiece and waited. "Hello, Sam," he said, "*wie gehts*?" Hawes listened, Byrnes listened, interjecting an occasional "Uh-huh" into the phone. He listened for about five minutes. Then he said, "Thanks a lot, Sam," and hung up.

"Anything?"

"A good set of prints on the glasses," Byrnes said. "Sam's already sent copies to the LB and to Washington. Keep your toes crossed. He's sending a written report back with the glasses. They're 1952 vintage, discontinued for the later models. Once we get them, I'll have Steve and Meyer start checking the hockshops. How about this Lady Astor? Think she's the target?"

Hawes shrugged. "I'll check her out."

"It could be," Byrnes said, returning the shrug. "What the hell? Person in the public eye. Maybe some jerk doesn't like the dirty songs she sings. What do you say?"

"I say it's worth a try."

"Make it fast," Byrnes said. "Don't stop to listen to any of her songs. We may have a few other tries to make before eight tonight." He looked at his watch. "Jesus, the time flies," he said.

A call to the Brisson Roof told Hawes that Jay Astor's first show went on at 8:00 P.M. The roof manager refused to divulge her address even when Hawes told him he was a detective. He insisted that Hawes give him a number to call back. Hawes gave him the Frederick 7 number, and the manager called back immediately, apparently satisfied after talking to the desk sergeant and being transferred to the Detective Division that he was talking to a bona fide cop and not one of Miss Astor's great unwashed. He gave Hawes the address, and Hawes left for the apartment immediately.

It seemed odd that Miss Astor was not staying at the hotel where she was performing, but perhaps she didn't like to mix business with pleasure. Her apartment was in uptown Isola, in the swank brownstone neighborhood on the south side, some thirty blocks below the first street in the 87th Precinct territory. Hawes made the drive in ten minutes. He left the car at the curb, climbed the twelve steps to the front door, and entered a small, immaculate lobby. He scanned the mailboxes. There was no Jay Astor listed on any of the boxes. He stepped outside and, standing on the front stoop once more, checked the address again. It was the right address. He went into the lobby again and rang for the superintendent. He could hear the loud bell sounding somewhere beyond the curtained inner-lobby door. He heard a door opening and closing, heard footsteps, and then the curtained door opened.

"Yes?" the man said. He was an old man wearing house-slippers and a faded-blue basque shirt.

"I'd like to see Miss Jay Astor," Hawes said.

"There's no Miss Astor here," the man answered.

"I'm not a fan or a reporter," Hawes said. "This is police business." He took out his wallet and opened it to his shield.

The man studied it. "You're a detective?" he asked.

"Yes."

"She's not in any trouble, is she?"

"She might be," Hawes said. "I'd like to talk to her."

"Just a minute," the man said. He went inside, leaving the curtained lobby door open, and also leaving the door to his ground-floor apartment ajar. Hawes could hear him dialing a phone. Upstairs, Hawes heard a phone ringing. The ringing stopped abruptly, and Hawes heard the old man talking. In a few minutes the old man came back.

"She said you should go up. It's Apartment 4-A. That's the one she uses for the entrance. She's got the whole top floor, actually. That's 4-A, 4-B, and 4-C. But she uses 4-A for the entrance, got the other ones blocked off from inside with furniture. 4-A. You can go right on up."

"Thank you," Hawes said. He moved past the old man into the hallway. Carpeted steps led from the inner hallway upstairs. An ornately carved banister was on one side of the steps. The hallway was suffocatingly hot. Hawes climbed the steps, thinking of Carella and Meyer hitting the hockshops. Would Byrnes ask for inter-precinct assistance on this one? Or did he expect the 87th to hit every hockshop in the city? No, he'd ask for other men. He'd have to.

There was a small placard set in a brass rectangle screwed to the doorjamb of Apartment 4-A. The placard simply read, ASTOR.

Hawes pressed the buzzer.

The door opened so rapidly that Hawes suspected Jay Astor had been standing just inside it

"You the detective?" she asked.

"Yes."

"Come in."

He walked into the apartment. If anything, Jay Astor was a disappointment. She had appeared sexy, slinky, and seductive in her newspaper photo, the skintight gown molding the abundant curves of a naturally endowed body. Her eyes had been provocative, and her smile had held the flash of promised evil, the tantalizing challenge of a mysterious woman. Here, in person, there was no challenge and no promise.

Jay Astor wore shorts and a halter. Her bosom was full and rich, but her legs were somewhat muscular, the legs of a tennis player. Her eyes were slightly squinted, but he realized instantly that the squint was a result of myopia and not sexuality. Her teeth revealed by her smile were rather large, giving her the appearance of a benevolent horse. Or perhaps he was being too cruel. He supposed, unprepared by the photo, he would have considered Miss Astor an attractive woman.

"The living room's air-conditioned," she said. "Come on in there, and we'll close the door."

He followed her into a room done in extreme modern. She closed the door behind him and said, "There. Isn't that better? This heat is the most. I came up from a South American tour two weeks ago, and believe me, it wasn't as hot down there. What can I do for you?"

"We received a letter this morning," Hawes said.

"Oh? What about?" Jay Astor went to the bar lining one side of the long room. "Would you like a drink? A gin rickey? A Tom Collins? You call it."

"Nothing, thanks."

Her face expressed mild surprise. Unperturbed, she began mixing herself a gin and tonic.

"The letter said, 'I will kill The Lady tonight at eight. What can you do about it?'" Hawes said.

"Nice letter." She pulled a face and squeezed a lime into the drink.

"You don't seem particularly impressed," Hawes said.

"Should I be?"

"You *are* known as 'The Lady,' aren't you?"

"Oh! Oh!" she said. "Oh, yes. The Lady. I will kill The Lady tonight. I see. Yes. Yes."

"Well?"

"A crank," Jay said.

"Maybe. Have you had any threatening letters or calls?"

"Recently, do you mean?"

"Yes."

"No, not recently. I get them every now and then. Jack the Ripper types. They call me smutty. They say they will kill me and cleanse the world in the blood of the lamb and like that. Buggos. Cranks." She turned from the bar, grinning. "I'm still alive."

"You seem to take all of it pretty lightly, Miss Astor."

"Call me Jay," she said. "I do. If I had to worry about every buggo who writes or calls, I'd become a buggo myself. There's no percentage in that."

"All the same, you *may* be the person indicated in this letter."

"So what do we do about it?"

"First of all, if you don't mind, we'd like to give you police protection tonight."

"All night?" Jay asked, raising an eyebrow coquettishly, her face expressing for a fleeting instant the promise and the challenge that was in the newspaper photo.

"Well, from when you leave the apartment until your show is over."

"My last show is at two," she said. "Your cop'll be busy. Or will the cop be you?"

"No, he won't," Hawes said.

"Worse luck," Jay answered, and she pulled at her drink.

"Your first show goes on at eight, is that right?"

"That's right."

"The letter says—"

"That could be a coincidence."

"Yes, it could. What time do you generally leave for the Brisson?"

"About seven."

"I'll have a patrolman stop by for you."

"A handsome Irish cop, I trust."

"We have a lot of those," Hawes said, smiling. "In the meantime, can you tell me whether or not anything has happened recently that would—"

"Cause someone to want me dead?" Jay thought for a moment. "No," she said.

"Anything at all? An argument? A contract dispute? A disgruntled musician? Anything?"

"No," she said pensively. "I'm easy to get along with. That's my rep in the trade. An easy lady," She grinned. "I didn't mean that to sound the way it did."

"How about the threatening letters and calls you mentioned? When was the last time you got one of those?"

"Oh, before I went to South America. That was months ago. I've only been back two weeks, you know. I doubt if the buggos know I'm around. When they hear my new album, they'll begin their poison penmanship again. Have you heard it?" She shook her head. "But of course you haven't. It hasn't been released yet."

She went to a hi-fi unit, opened one of the cabinets, and pulled a record album from the top shelf. On the album cover,

Lady Astor was riding a white horse, naked. Her long black hair had been released so that it cascaded over her breasts, effectively covering her. There was the same malevolent, mischievous, inviting gleam in her eyes as had been in the newspaper photo. The album was titled *Astor's Pet Horse*.

"It's a collection of cowboy songs," Jay explained, "with the lyrics jazzed up a bit. Would you like to hear a little of it?"

"Well, I—"

"It won't take a minute," Jay said, moving to the hi-fi and putting the record on the turntable. "You'll be getting a sneak preview. What other detective in the city can make that statement?"

"I wanted to—"

"Sit," Jay said, and the record began.

It began with the customary corny cowboy guitar, and then Lady Aster's insinuatingly chic voice came smoothly over the speaker.

"Home, home in the slums," she sang.

"Full of pushers, and junkies, and bums.

"Where seldom is heard

"Mating call of the bird,

"And the zip guns play music like drums..."

The record went on and on. Hawes thought it only mildly funny. He was too close to the reality to find the parody amusing. At the end of "Home on the Range," a parody of "Deep in the Heart of Texas" began.

"This one is a little rough," Jay said, "full of innuendo. A lot of people won't like it, but I don't give a damn. Morality is a funny thing, do you know?"

"How do you mean?"

"I came to the conclusion a long time ago that morality is strictly personal. The hardest thing any artist can attempt is to reconcile his own moral standards with those of the great unwashed. It can't be done. Morality is morality, and mine's mine, and yours is yours. There are things I accept matter-of-factly, and these same things shock the hell out of the Kansas City housewife. That's a trap the artist can fall into."

"What trap?"

"Most artists—in show business, anyway—live in the big cities. That's where the business is, you know, so that's where you have to be. Well, urban morality is pretty different from morality in the sticks. The stuff that goes with the city slickers just won't go with the guy mowing a field of wheat—or whatever the hell you do with wheat. But if you try to please everybody, you go buggo. So I try to please myself. If I use my own good taste, I figure the morals will take care of themselves."

"And do they?"

"Sometimes, yes; sometimes, no. Like I said, things I consider absolutely pure and simple don't seem quite so pure or quite so simple to the farmhand."

"Things like what?" Hawes asked innocently.

"Things like—would you like to go to bed with me?"

"Yes, I would," he answered automatically.

"Then let's," she said, putting down her drink.

"Right now?" he asked.

"Why not? It's as good a time as any."

He felt ridiculous answering what he had to answer, but he plunged ahead, anyway. "I haven't the time right now," he said.

"Your letter-sender?"

"My letter-sender."

"You may have lost your golden opportunity," she said.

"Those are the breaks," Hawes said, shrugging.

"Morality is a question of the means and the opportunity," Jay said.

"Like murder," Hawes answered.

"If you want to get morbid, okay. All I'm trying to say is that I would like you to make love to me now. Tomorrow I may not feel the same way. I may not even feel the same way ten minutes from now."

"Now you've spoiled it," Hawes said.

Jay raised an eyebrow inquisitively.

"I thought it was me. Instead, it's just your whim of the moment."

"What do you want me to do? Undress you and burp you?"

"No," Hawes said, rising. "Give me a rain check."

"It hasn't rained for weeks," Jay said.

"Maybe it will."

"And to quote an old sawhorse, 'Lightning never strikes twice in the same place.'"

"I'll tell you," Hawes said, "I'm just liable to go out and shoot myself."

Jay smiled. "You're pretty damned sure of yourself, aren't you?"

"Am I?" he asked.

For a moment they faced each other. There was none of the photographic sensuality on her face now. Neither was there the fury of a woman scorned. There was only the somewhat pathetic loneliness of a little girl living in a vast top-floor apartment with an air-conditioner in the living room.

Lady Astor shrugged.

"What the hell," she said, "Give me a call sometime. The whim may return."

"Expect that cop," Hawes said.

"I will," she answered. "He may beat your time."

Hawes shrugged philosophically. "Some guys have all the luck," he said, and he left the apartment.

Some guys, too, have all the misfortune.

Meyer Meyer and Steve Carella had their share that blistering day. By 1:40 P.M. the sidewalks were baking, the buildings were ready to turn cherry red with contained heat, the people were wilting, automobile tires were melting, and it was obvious even to the neophyte science fiction fan that the earth had somehow wandered too close to the sun. It would surely be consumed by fire. This was the last day, and Richard Matheson had called the tune, and the world would end in molten fire.

Undramatically speaking, it was damn hot.

Meyer Meyer was a sweater. He sweated even in the wintertime. He didn't know why he sweated. He supposed it was a nervous reaction. But he was always covered with perspiration. Today he was drowning in it. As the two detectives wandered from hockshop to hockshop on sleazy Crichton Avenue, wandered from open door to open door, passed rapidly from one trio of gold balls to the next, Meyer thought he would die in a way unbefitting a heroic cop. He would die of heat prostration, and the obits would simply say, COP FLOPS. Or perhaps, if the news was headlined in *Variety*, SOPPY COP DROPS.

"How do you like this *Variety* headline announcing my death by heat prostration?" he said to Carella as they entered another hockshop, "Soppy Cop Drops."

"That's pretty good," Carella said. "How about mine?"

"In *Variety*?"

"Sure.

"Let me hear it."

"Soppy Wop Cop Drops."

Meyer burst out laughing. "You're a prejudiced bastard," he said.

The owner of the hockshop looked up as they approached his cage.

"Yes, sir, gentlemen," he said, "what can I do for you, sirs?"

"We're from the police," Carella said. He plunked the binoculars down on the countertop. "Recognize these?"

The hockshop owner examined them. "A beautiful pair of glasses," he said. "Pieter-Vondiger. Have they figured in a crime, perhaps?"

"They have."

"Was the perpetrator carrying them?"

"He was."

"Mmmm," the owner said.

"Recognize them?"

"We sell a lot of field glasses. That is, when we have them to sell."

"Did you have *these* to sell?"

"I don't think so. The last Pieter-Vondigers I had was in January. These are eight by thirty. The pair I had were six by thirty. These are better glasses."

"Then you didn't sell these glasses?"

"No, sirs, I didn't. Are they stolen?"

"Not according to our lists."

"I'm sorry I can't help you, sirs."

"That's all right," Carella said. "Thanks."

They walked out onto the blistering sidewalk again.

"How many other cops are on this?" Meyer asked.

"Pete asked for a pair from each precinct. Maybe they'll come up with something."

"I'm getting tired. Do you suppose that damn letter is a phony?"

"I don't know. If it is, we ought to lock the bastard up, anyway."

"Hear, hear," Meyer said, in a burst of enthusiasm rare for the heat.

"Maybe we'll get a make on the prints," Carella said.

"Sure, maybe," Meyer agreed. "Maybe it'll rain."

"Maybe," Carella said.

They walked into the next shop. There were two men behind the counter. Both grinned as Meyer and Carella crossed the room.

"Good afternoon," one said, smiling.

"A pleasant day," the other said, smiling.

"I'm Jason Bloom," the first said.

"I'm Jacob Bloom," echoed the other.

"How do you do?" Carella answered. "We're Detectives Meyer and Carella of the 87th Squad."

"A pleasure, gentlemen," Jason said.

"Welcome to our shop," Jacob said.

"We're trying to trace the owner of these binoculars," Carella said. He put them on the counter. "Do you recognize them?"

"Pieter-Vondiger," Jason said.

"Excellent glasses," Jacob said.

"Superb."

"Magnificent."

Carella broke into the lavish praise. "Recognize them?"

"Pieter-Vondiger," Jason said. "Didn't we—"

"Precisely," Jacob said.

"The man with the—"

And the brothers burst out laughing together. Carella and Meyer waited. The laughter showed no signs of subsiding. It was reaching heights of hysteria, unprecedented hurricanes of hilarity, fits of festivity. Still, the detectives waited. At last the laughter subsided.

"Oh my God," Jason said, chuckling.

"Do we remember these glasses?"

"Do we?" Jason said.

"Oh my God," Jacob said.

"Do you?" Carella asked. He was hot.

Jason sobered instantly. "*Are* these the glasses, Jacob?" he asked.

"Certainly," Jacob said.

"But are you sure?"

"The scratch on the side, don't you remember? See, there is the scratch. Don't you remember he complained about the scratch? We reduced the glasses a dollar and a quarter because of the scratch. And all the while he was—" Jacob burst out laughing again.

"Oh my God," Jason said, laughing with him.

Meyer looked at Carella. Carella looked at Meyer. Apparently the heat in the shop had grown too intense for the brothers.

Carella cleared his throat. Again the laughter subsided.

"Did you sell these glasses to someone?" he asked.

"Yes," Jason said.

"Certainly," Jacob said.

"Who?"

"The man with the lollipop!" Jason said, bursting into a new gale of hysteria.

"The man with the lollipop!" Jacob repeated, unable to keep his laugh from booming out of his mouth.

"This man had a lollipop?" Carella asked, deadpanned.

Yes, yes! Oh my God!"

"He was sucking on it all the while we haggled over the... the..."

"...the glasses," Jason concluded. "Oh my God. Oh my good Lord! When he left the shop, we couldn't stop laughing. Do you remember, Jacob?"

"Yes, yes, how could I forget? A red lollipop! Oh, was he enjoying it! Oh, no child ever enjoyed a lollipop more! It was wonderful! Wonderful!"

"Magnificent!" Jason said.

"Fantastically—"

"What was his name?" Carella asked.

"Who?" Jason asked, sobering.

"The man with the lollipop."

"Oh, what was his name, Jacob?"

"I don't know, Jason."

Carella looked at Meyer. Meyer looked at Carella.

"Isn't there a bill of sale, Jacob?"

"Certainly, Jason."

"When was he here?"

"Two weeks ago, wasn't it?"

"A Friday?"

"No, a Saturday. No, you're right, it was a Friday."

"When was that? What date?"

"I don't know. Where's the calendar?" The brothers busied themselves over a calendar on the wall.

"There," Jacob said, pointing.

"Yes," Jason agreed.

"Friday," Jacob said.

"July twelfth."

"Would you check your bills?" Carella asked.

"Certainly."

"Of course."

The brothers moved into the back room.

"Nice," Meyer said.

"What?"

"Brotherly love."

"Um," Carella answered.

The brothers returned with a yellow carbon copy of the bill.

"Here it is," Jason said.

"July twelfth, just as we thought."

"And the man's name?" Carella asked.

"M. Samalson," Jason said.

"No first name?"

"Just the initial," Jason said.

"We only take the initial," Jacob corroborated.

"Any address?" Meyer asked.

"Can you read this?" Jason asked, indicating the writing on the line printed *Address:*.

"It's your handwriting."

"No, no, you wrote it," Jason said.

"You did," Jacob told him. "See how the *t* is crossed. That is your handwriting."

"Possibly. But what does it say?"

"That's a *t*, for sure," Jacob said.

"Yes. Oh, it's Calm's Point! Of course! That's Calm's Point."

"But what's the address?"

"3163 Jefferson Street, Calm's Point," Jason said, in a deciphering burst.

Meyer copied down the address.

"A lollipop!" Jason said.

"Oh my God," Jacob said.

"Thank you very much for..." Carella started, but the brothers were laughing to beat the band, so the two detectives simply left the shop.

"Calm's Point," Carella said when they were outside. "Clear the hell over on the other end of the city."

"It would be that way," Meyer said.

"We'd better get back to the squad. Pete may want to put a Calm's Point precinct on it."

"Right," Meyer said. They walked back to the car. "You want to drive?"

"I don't care. You tired?"

"No. No. I just thought you might want to drive."

"Okay," Carella said.

They got into the car.

"Think those reports on the prints are back yet?"

"I hope so. Might save us a call to Calm's Point."

"Um," Meyer said.

They set the car in motion. They were silent for a while. Then Meyer said, "Steve, it's hot as hell today."

The reports from the Bureau of Criminal Identification and the FBI were waiting at the office when Carella and Meyer returned. Both agencies had reported that they were unable to find fingerprints in their vast files corresponding to the ones taken from the binoculars.

Hawes walked into the squadroom as the men were reading the reports.

"Any luck?" he asked.

"No make," Carella said. "But we got the name of the guy who bought those binoculars. That's a break."

"Pete want to pick him up?"

"I haven't told him yet."

"What's his name?"

"M. Samalson."

"You'd better tell Pete quick," Hawes said. "I got a good look at the guy who slugged me. If it was Samalson, I'll know it."

"And we've also got the prints to compare, in case your memory's faulty," Carella said. He paused. "How'd you make out with Lady Astor?"

Hawes winked and said nothing.

Carella sighed and went into Byrnes's office.

The closest Calm's Point precinct to M. Samalson's home address was the 102nd. Byrnes put in a call to the detective squad there and asked them to pick up and deliver Samalson as soon as possible.

At 2:00 P.M. a new batch of kids in dungarees and red-striped T-shirts was trotted into the precinct squadroom. Dave Murchison was brought up from the desk. He looked the kids over, stopped before one of them, and said, "This is the kid."

Byrnes walked over to the boy.

"Did you deliver a letter here this morning?" he asked.

"No," the boy said.

"He's the kid," Murchison insisted.

"What's your name, son?" Byrnes asked.

"Frankie Annuci."

"Did you bring a letter here this morning?"

"No," the kid said.

"Did you come into the building and ask for the desk sergeant?"

"No," the kid said.

"Did you hand a letter to this man here?" Byrnes said, indicating Murchison.

"No," the kid said.

"He's lying," Murchison said. "This is the kid."

"Come on, Frankie," Byrnes said gently. "You did deliver that letter, didn't you?"

"No."

There was fear in the boy's wide blue eyes, fear of the law, a fear deeply ingrained in the mind of every precinct citizen.

"You're not in any trouble, son," Byrnes said. "We're trying to find the man who gave you that letter. Now, you did deliver it, didn't you?"

"No," the kid said.

Byrnes turned to the other detectives, his patience beginning to wear thin. Hawes walked to the boy, joining Byrnes.

"You've got nothing to be afraid of, Frankie. We're trying to find the man who gave you that letter, do you understand? Now, where did you first meet him?"

"I didn't meet anybody," the kid said.

"Get rid of the rest of these kids, Meyer," Byrnes said. Meyer began shuttling the other boys out of the room. Frankie Annuci watched their departure, his eyes growing wider.

"How about it, Frankie?" Carella asked. Unconsciously, he had drifted into the circle around the boy. When Meyer had got rid of the other boys, he came back to stand with Byrnes, Hawes, and Carella. There was something amusing about the scene. The ridiculousness of it struck each of the detectives at the same moment. They had automatically assumed the formation for intense interrogation, but their victim was a boy no older than ten, and they felt somewhat like bullies as they surrounded him, ready to fire their questions in machine-gun bursts. And yet, this boy was a possible lead to the man they were seeking, a lead that might prove more fruitful than the thus far phantom name of M. Samalson. They waited, as if unwilling to begin the barrage until their commanding officer gave the signal to fire.

Byrnes opened it.

"Now, we're going to ask some questions, Frankie," he said gently, "and we want you to answer them. All right?"

"All right," Frankie said.

"Who gave you the letter?"

"Nobody."

"Was it a man?"

"I don't know."

"A woman?" Hawes asked.

"I don't know."

"Do you know what the letter said?" Carella asked.

"No."

"Did you open it?" Meyer said.

"No."

"But there *was* a letter?"

"No."

"You did deliver a letter?"

"No."

"You're lying, aren't you?"

"No."

"Where'd you meet the man?"

"I didn't meet anybody."

"Near the park?"

"No."

"The candy store?"

"No."

"One of the side streets?"

"No."

"Was he driving a car?"

"No."

"There *was* a man?"

"I don't know."

"Was he a man or a woman?"

"I don't know."

"The letter said he was going to kill somebody tonight. Did you know that?"

"No."

"Would you like this man or this woman to kill somebody?"

"No."

"Well, he's going to kill somebody. That's what the letter said. He's going to kill a lady."

"She may be your mother, Frankie."

"Would you like this man to kill your mother?"

"No," Frankie said.

"Then tell us who he is. We want to stop him."

"I don't know who he is!" Frankie blurted.

"You never saw him before today?"

Frankie began crying. "No," he said. "Never."

"What happened, Frankie?" Carella asked, handing the boy his handkerchief.

Frankie dabbed at his eyes and then blew his nose. "He just came over to me, that's all," he said. "I didn't know he was gonna kill anybody. I swear to God!"

"We know you didn't know, Frankie. Was he on foot or in a car?"

"A car."

"What make?"

"I don't know."

"What color?"

"Blue."

"A convertible."

"No."

"A sedan?"

"What's a sedan?"

"Hardtop."

"Yes."

"Did you see the license number?"

"No."

"What happened, Frankie?"

"He called me over to the car. My mother said I should never get in cars with strangers, but he didn't want me to get in the car. He asked me if I wanted to make five bucks."

"What did you say?"

"I said how?"

"Go ahead, Frankie," Byrnes said.

"He said I should take this letter to the police station around the corner."

"What street were you on, Frankie?"

"Seventh. Right around the corner."

"Okay. Go ahead."

"He said I should come in and ask for the desk sergeant and then give it to him and leave."

"Did he give you the five dollars then or later?"

"Right then," Frankie said. "With the letter."

"Have you still got it?" Byrnes asked.

"I spent some of it."

"We wouldn't get anything from a bill, anyway," Meyer said.

"No," Byrnes said. "Did you get a good look at this man, Frankie?"

"Pretty good."

"Can you describe him?"

"Well, he had short hair."

"Very short?"

"Pretty short."

"What color eyes?"

"Blue, I think. They were light, anyway."

"Any scars you could see?"

"No."

"Mustache?"

"No."

"What was he wearing?"

"A yellow sports shirt," Frankie said.

"That's our man," Hawes put in. "That's who I tangled with in the park."

"I want a police artist up here," Byrnes said. "Meyer, get one, will you? If this Samalson doesn't work out, we may be able to use a picture to show around." He turned sharply. The phone in his office was ringing. "Just a second, Frankie," he said, and he went into the office and answered the phone.

When he returned, he said, "That was the 102nd. They checked Samalson's home address. He isn't there. His landlady says he works in Isola."

"Where?" Carella asked.

"A few blocks from here. A supermarket called Beaver Brothers, Inc. Do you know it?"

"I'm halfway there," Carella said.

On the telephone, Meyer Meyer said, "This is the 87th Squad. Lieutenant Byrnes wants an artist up here right away. Can you—"

Cotton Hawes knew the instant Carella brought the man into the squadroom that he was not the man who'd assaulted him in the park.

Martin Samalson was a tall, thin man wearing the white apron of a supermarket clerk, the apron somehow emphasizing his gauntness. His hair was blond and wavy and worn long. His eyes were brown.

"What do you say, Cotton?" Byrnes asked.

"Not him," Hawes said.

"Is this the man who gave you the letter, Frankie?"

"No," Frankie said.

"What letter?" Samalson asked, wiping his hands on the apron.

Byrnes picked up the binoculars, which were resting on Carella's desk. "These yours?" he asked.

Samalson looked at them in surprise. "Yeah! Hey, how about that? Where'd you find them?"

"Where'd you lose them?" Byrnes asked.

Samalson seemed suddenly aware of the situation. "Hey, now wait a minute, just wait a minute! I lost those glasses last Sunday. I don't know why you dragged me in here, but if it's got something to do with those glasses, just forget it! Boy, get off that kick fast." He shook the air with one outstretched palm, wiping the slate clean.

"When did you buy them?" Byrnes asked.

"About two weeks ago. A hockshop on Crichton. You can check it."

"We already have," Byrnes said. "We know all about the lollipop."

"Huh?"

"You went into the shop sucking a lollipop."

"Oh." Samalson looked sheepish. "I had a sore throat. It's good to keep your mouth wet when you got a sore throat. That's why I had the lollipop. There's no law against that."

"And you had these glasses until last Sunday, is that right? And last Sunday you claim you lost them."

"That's right."

"Sure you didn't loan them to anybody?"

"Positive. Last Sunday I went on a boat ride. Up the Harb. That's when I musta lost them. I don't know what them damn glasses have been doing since, and I don't care. You can't tie me up with them after last Sunday. Damn right!"

"Slow down, Samalson," Hawes said.

"Slow down, my ass! You drag me into a police station and—"

"I said slow down!" Hawes said. Samalson looked at his face. Instantly, he shut up.

"What boat were you on last Sunday?" Hawes asked, the menace still in his voice and on his face.

"The SS *Alexander*," Samalson said pettishly.

"Where'd it go?"

"Up the River Harb. To Paisley Mountain."

"When'd you lose the glasses?"

"It must've been on the way back. I had them while we were at the picnic grounds."

"You think you lost them on the boat?"

"Maybe. I don't know."

"Did you go anywhere afterward?"

"How do you mean?"

"After the boat docked?"

"Yeah. I was with a girl. The boat docks right near here, you know. On North Twenty-fifth. I had my car parked there. So we drove down to a bar near the supermarket. I stop there every now and then on my way home from work. That's how come I was familiar with it. I didn't feel like tracking all over the city looking for a nice place."

"What's the name of the bar?"

"The Pub."

"Where is it?"

"It's on North Thirteenth, Pete," Carella said. "I know the place. It's pretty nice for this neighborhood."

"Yeah, it's a nice bar," Samalson agreed. "I took the girl there, and then we drove around for a while."

"Did you park?"

"Yes."

"Where?"

"Near her house. In Riverhead."

"Could you have lost the glasses then?"

"I suppose so. I think I lost them on the boat, though."

"Could you have lost them in this bar?"

"Maybe. But I think it was the boat."

"Come here, Steve," Byrnes said, and both men walked toward Byrnes's office. In a whisper, Byrnes asked, "What do you think? Should we hold him?"

"What for?"

"Hell, he may be an accomplice in this thing. That lost-glasses story stinks to high heaven."

"It doesn't read like a pair, Pete. I think our killer is a single."

"Still, the killer may know him. May head for this guy's place after the murder. Put a tail on him. O'Brien's sitting at his desk doing nothing. Use him." Byrnes walked back to Samalson. Carella walked over to where Bob O'Brien was typing a report at the other end of the squadroom. He began talking to him in a whisper. O'Brien nodded.

"You can go, Samalson," Byrnes said. "Don't try to leave the city. We may want to question you further."

"Would anyone mind telling me what the hell this is about?" Samalson said.

"Yes, we would," Byrnes said.

"Boy, some goddamn police department in this city," Samalson said, fuming. "Can I have my glasses back?"

"We're finished with them," Byrnes said.

"Thanks for nothing," Samalson said, seizing the glasses. Hawes led him to the railing and watched as he went down the steps, still fuming. O'Brien left the squadroom a moment later.

"Can I go, too?" Frankie asked.

"Not yet, son," Byrnes said. "We're going to need you in a little while."

"What for?" Frankie asked.

"We're going to draw a picture," Byrnes said. "Miscolo!" he yelled.

From the clerical office outside the railing, Miscolo's head appeared. "Yo?" he said.

"You got any milk in there?"

"Sure."

"Get this kid a glass, will you? And some cookies. You want some cookies, Frankie?"

Frankie nodded. Byrnes tousled his hair and went back into the corner office.

At 2:39 P.M. the police artist arrived.

He did not look at all like an artist. He did not wear a smock or a floppy bow tie, and his fingers were not stained with paint. He wore rimless eyeglasses, and he looked like a bored salesman for an exterminating service.

"You jokers send for an artist?" he asked at the railing, resting his leather case on the wood.

Hawes looked up. "Yes," he said. "Come on in."

The man pushed his way through the gate. "George Angelo," he said, extending his hand. "No relation to Michel, either family-wise or talent-wise." He grinned, exposing large white teeth. "Who do you want sketched?"

"A ghost," Hawes said. "This kid and I both saw him. We'll give you the description, you make the picture. Deal?"

"Deal," Angelo said, nodding. "I hope you both saw the same ghost."

"We did," Hawes said.

"And can both describe him the same way. I sometimes get twelve eyewitnesses who each saw the same guy twelve different ways. You'd be surprised how cockeyed the average citizen is." He shrugged. "But you're a trained observer, and kids are innocent and unprejudiced, so who knows? Maybe this'll be a good one."

"Where do you want to set up?" Hawes asked.

"Anyplace you got light," Angelo answered. "How about that desk near the window?"

"Fine," Hawes said. He turned to the boy. "Frankie, want to come over here?"

They walked to the desk. Angelo opened his case. "This going into the newspapers?"

"No."

"Television?"

"No. We haven't got time for that. We just want copies run off for the men trying to track down this guy."

"Okay," Angelo said. He reached into the case for a sketch pad and pencil. Then he took out a stack of rectangular cards. He sat at the desk, looked up at the sunlight once, and then nodded.

"Where do you want us to start?"

"Pick the shape of the face from the shapes on this card," Angelo said. "Square, oval, triangular, they're all there. Look them over."

Hawes and Frankie studied the card. "Something like this, don't you think?" Hawes asked the kid.

"Yeah, something like that," Frankie agreed.

"The oval?" Angelo asked. "Okay, we'll start with that."

Quickly, he sketched an egg-shaped outline on the pad. "How about noses? See anything here that looks like his nose?" He produced another card. Hawes and Frankie looked at the profusion of smellers that covered the card.

"None of them look just like his nose," Frankie said.

"Any of them come close?"

"Well, maybe this one. But not really."

"The idea in this is simplicity," Angelo said to Hawes. "We're not trying for a portrait that'll hang in the Louvre. We want a likeness that people can identify. Shade and shadow tend to confuse. I try to stick to line, blacks and whites, a feeling of the person rather than a photographic representation. So if you'll try to remember the characteristics that struck you most about this man, I'll try to get them on paper—simply. We'll refine as we go along. This is just the beginning; we'll draw and we'll draw until we get something that looks like him. Now, how about those noses? Which one is the closest to his?"

"This, I guess," the kid said. Hawes agreed.

"Okay." Angelo began sketching. He produced another card. "Eyes?"

"He had blue eyes, I remember that," Hawes said. "Sort of slanted, downward."

"Yeah," the kid said. Angelo kept nodding and drawing.

The first sketch looked like this:

"That don't look like him at all," the kid said when Angelo showed it.

"All right," Angelo said mildly. "Tell me what's wrong with it."

"It just don't look like the guy, that's all."

"Well, where is it wrong?"

"I don't know," the kid said, shrugging.

"He's too young, for one thing," Hawes said. "The guy we saw is an older man. Late thirties, maybe early forties."

"Okay. Start with the top of the picture and work your way down. What's wrong with it?"

"He's got too much hair," the kid said.

"Yes," Hawes agreed. "Or maybe too much head."

Angelo began erasing. "That better?"

"Yeah, but he was going bald a little," the kid said, "like up here. On the forehead."

Angelo erased two sharp wings into the black hair on the man's forehead. "What else?"

"His eyebrows were thicker," Hawes said.

"What else?"

"His nose was shorter," the kid said.

"Or maybe the space between his nose and his mouth was longer, either one," Hawes said. "But what you've got doesn't look right."

"Good, good," Angelo said. "Go on."

"His eyes looked sleepier."

"More slanted?"

"No. Heavier lids."

They watched as Angelo sketched. Putting an overlay of tracing paper onto the erased drawing, he began to move his pencil rapidly, nodding to himself as he worked, his tongue peeking from one corner of his mouth. At last he looked up.

"This any better?" he asked.

He showed them the second drawing:

"It still don't look like him," Frankie said.

"What's wrong?" Angelo asked.

"He's still too young," Hawes said.

"Also, he looks like a devil. His hair is too sharp," Frankie said.

"The hairline, you mean?"

"Yeah. It looks like he got horns. That's wrong."

"Go ahead."

"The nose is about the right length now," Hawes said, "but it's still not the right shape. He had more of a—this middle thing, whatever you call it, the thing between the nostrils."

"The tip of his nose? Longer?"

"Yes."

"How are the eyes?" Angelo asked. "Better?"

"The eyes look right," Frankie said. "Don't touch the eyes. Don't them eyes look right?"

"Yes," Hawes said. "The mouth is wrong."

"What's wrong with it?"

"It's too small. He had a wide mouth."

"And thin," the kid said. "Thin lips."

"Is the cleft chin right?" Angelo asked.

"Yeah, the chin looks okay. But that hair..." Angelo was beginning to fill in the hairline with his pencil. "That's better, yeah, that's better."

"A widow's peak?" Angelo asked. "Like this?"

"Not as pronounced," Hawes said. "He had very close-cropped hair, receding above the temples, but not as pronounced as that. Yes, now you're getting it, that's closer."

"The mouth longer and thinner, right?" Angelo asked, and his pencil moved furiously. Working with a new sheet of tracing paper, he began to transpose results of the collaboration. It was very hot at the desk where he worked. His sweating fist stuck to the flimsy tracing paper.

The third version of the suspect looked like this:

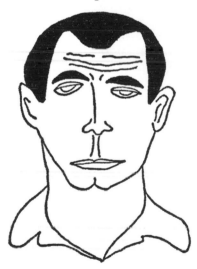

There was a fourth version, and a fifth version, and a tenth version, and a twelfth version, and still Angelo worked at the desk in the sunlight. Hawes and the boy kept correcting him, often changing their minds after they had seen their verbal description

take shape on paper. Angelo was a skilled technician who trans-
posed their every word into simple line. Their reversals of opinion
did not seem to disturb him. Patiently, he listened. And patiently,
he corrected.

"It's getting worse," the kid said. "It don't look at all like him
now. It looked better in the beginning."

"Change the nose," Hawes said. "It had a hook in it. Right in
the middle. As if it had been broken."

"More spaces between the nose and the mouth."

"Shaggier eyebrows. Heavier."

"Lines under the eyes."

"Lines coming from his nose."

"Older. Make him older."

"Make his mouth a little crooked."

"No, straighter."

"Better, better."

Angelo worked. There was sweat clinging to his forehead.
They tried turning on the fan once, but it blew Angelo's papers
all over the floor. From time to time, cops from all over the precinct drifted over to where Angelo was working at the desk. They
stopped behind him, looking over his shoulder.

"That's pretty good," one of them said, never having seen the
suspect in question.

The floor was covered with sheets of rumpled tracing paper
now. Still Hawes and Frankie fired their impressions of the
man they had seen, and Angelo faithfully tried to capture those
impressions on paper. And suddenly, after they had lost count of
the number of drawings, Hawes said, "Hold it! That's it."

"That's him," the kid said. "That's the guy!"

"Don't change a line," Hawes said. "You've got him! That's the
man." The kid grinned from ear to ear and then shook hands with
Hawes.

Angelo sighed a heavy sigh of relief.

This was the picture they felt resembled the man they had both seen:

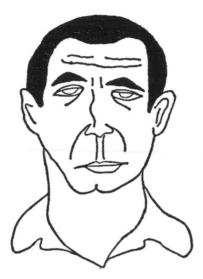

Angelo began packing his case.

"That's very neat," the kid said.

"That's my signature," Angelo replied. "Neat. Forget this Angelo stuff. My real name is Neat, with a capital *N*." He grinned. He seemed very happy it was all over.

"How soon can we get copies?" Hawes asked.

"How soon do you need them?"

Hawes looked at his watch. "It's three-fifteen," he said. "This guy is going to kill a woman at eight tonight."

Angelo nodded seriously, the cop in him momentarily replacing the artist. "Send a man with me," he said. "I'll run them off the minute I get back."

At 4:05 P.M., armed with pictures the ink on which was still wet, Carella and Hawes left the precinct simultaneously, Carella headed for a bar on North Thirteenth, a bar named The Pub, the bar to which Samalson had taken his girl on the preceding Sunday. Carella went there solely to show the picture to the bartender in the hope he might identify the suspect.

Hawes went directly around the corner from the precinct to Seventh Street, where Frankie Annuci had said he had met the man who'd given him the letter. It was Hawes's plan to start with Seventh and work his way east, heading uptown, going as far as Thirty-third if he had to. He would then double-back, working north and south. If the man lived anywhere in the neighborhood, Hawes meant to find him. In the meantime, a copy of the picture had been sent to the IB in the hope of getting a make from the photos in the files in case none of the investigating cops struck pay dirt.

At 4:10 P.M. Meyer and Willis left the squadroom with their copies of the picture. Starting with Sixth Street, their plan was to work westward from the precinct, going down past First and into the named streets below First until they hit Lady Astor's street.

At 4:15 P.M. a squad car was called back to the precinct. Copies of the picture were dumped into the car and then distributed to every motorized and foot patrolman in the precinct. Copies were delivered to the neighboring 88th and 89th Precincts, too. The immediate area adjacent to the precinct, starting with Grover Avenue and going into Grover Park, was flooded with detectives from the 88th and the 89th (which precincts handled the actual park territory), in the event the suspect might return in search of his binoculars. It was a big city, and a big, teeming precinct—but the precinct was fortunately smaller than the city.

Hawes, stopping at every store, stopping at every tenement, talking to shop owners and superintendents, talking to the kids in the streets, who were sometimes the shrewdest observers around, did not connect until he reached Twelfth Street.

It was late afternoon by this time, but the streets had not cooled down at all. Hawes was still hot, and he was beginning to feel the first disgruntled disappointment of defeat. How the hell would they ever stop this guy? How the hell would they ever find him? Dispiritedly, he began working his way up the street, showing the picture. No, they did not know the man. No, they did not recognize him. Was he from the neighborhood?

At the fifth tenement from the corner, he showed the picture to a landlady in a flowered cotton housedress.

"No," she said instantly. "I never—" And then she stopped. She took the picture from Hawes's hands. "Yeah, that's him," she said. "That's the way he looked this morning. I saw him when he was coming down. That's the way he looked."

"Who?" Hawes said. He could feel the sudden surge of energy within him as he waited for her answer.

"Smith," she said. "John Smith. A weird duck. He had this—"

"What apartment?" Hawes said.

"22. That's on the second floor. He moved in about two weeks ago. Had this—"

But Hawes was already moving into the building, his gun drawn. He did not know that his conversation with the landlady had been viewed from a second-floor window. He did not know that his red hair had instantly identified him to his observer. He did not know until he was almost on the second-floor landing, and then he knew instantly.

The explosion thundered in the small, narrow corridor. Hawes fell to the floor at once, almost losing his footing on the top step, almost hurtling backward down the stairwell. He fired a shot into the dimness, not seeing anything, but wanting John Smith to know he was armed.

"Get out of here, cop!" the voice shouted.

"Throw your gun down here," Hawes said. "There are four cops with me downstairs. You haven't got a chance."

"You're a liar," the man shouted. "I saw you when you got here. You came alone. I saw you from the window."

Another shot exploded into the hallway. Hawes ducked below the top step. The bullet ripped plaster from the already chipped plaster on the wall. He squinted his eyes, trying to see into the dimness, cursing his position. Wherever Smith was, he could see Hawes without, in turn, being seen. Hawes could not move from his uncomfortable position on the steps. But perhaps Smith couldn't move, either. Perhaps if he left wherever he was, he would be seen. Hawes waited.

The hall went utterly still.

"Smith?" he called.

A fusillade of shots answered him, angry shots that whined across the hallway and ripped at the plaster. Chalk cascaded onto Hawes's head. He clung to the steps, cursing tenement hallways and would-be killers. From the street below, he could hear excited yells and screams, and then the repeated, shouted word "Police! Police! Police! Police!"

"Do you hear that, Smith?" he shouted. "They're calling the cops. The whole damn precinct'll be here in three minutes. Throw your gun down."

Smith fired again. The shot was lower. It ripped a splinter of wood from the landing near the top step. Hawes reared back and then instantly ducked. He heard a clicking at the other end of the hallway. Smith was reloading. He was about to sprint down the corridor when he heard a clip being slammed into the butt of an automatic. Quickly, he ducked down behind the top step again.

The hallway was silent again.

"Smith?"

There was no answer.

"Smith?"

From the street below, Hawes heard the high whine of a police siren.

"You hear that, Smith? They're here. They'll be—"

Three shots exploded into the hallway. Hawes ducked and then heard a man scuffling to his feet, caught a glimpse of a trouser leg as Smith started up the stairway. Hawes bounded into the hallway, triggering a shot at the retreating figure. Smith turned and fired, and Hawes dropped to the floor again. The footsteps were clattering up the steps now, noisily, excitedly, hurriedly. Hawes got to his feet, ran for the steps, charged up them two at a time. Another shot spun into the hallway. He did not duck this time. He kept charging up the steps, wanting to reach Smith before he got to the roof. He heard the roof door being tried, heard Smith pounding on it, and then heard a shot and the spanging reverberation of metal exploding. The roof door creaked open and then slammed shut. Smith was already on the roof.

Hawes rushed up the remaining steps. A skylight threw bright sunshine on the landing inside the roof door. He opened the door and then closed it again rapidly when a bullet ripped into the jamb, splashing wood splinters onto his face.

Goddamn you! he thought. *You goddamn son of a bitch, goddamn you!*

He threw open the door, fired a blind fusillade of shots across the roof, and then followed his own cover out onto the melting tar. He saw a figure dart behind one of the chimney pots and then rush for the parapet at the roof's edge. He fired. His shot was high. He was not shooting to warn or to wound now. He was shooting to kill. Smith rose for an instant, poised on the edge of the roof. Hawes fired, and Smith leaped the airshaft between the buildings, landing behind the parapet on the adjoining roof. Hawes started after him, his shoes sticking in the tar. He reached the edge of the roof. He hesitated just an instant and then leaped the airshaft, landing on his hands and knees in the sticky tar.

Smith had already crossed the roof. He looked back, fired at Hawes, and then rushed for the ledge. Hawes leveled his revolver. Smith climbed onto the ledge, silhouetted against the painful blue of the sky, and Hawes steadied the revolver on his left arm, taking careful aim. He knew that if Smith got onto that next roof, if Smith maintained the lead he now had, he would get away. And so he took careful aim, knowing that this shot had to count, watching Smith as he raised his arms in preparation for his jump across the airshaft. He aimed for the section of trunk that presented the widest target. He did not want to miss.

Smith stood undecided on the ledge for a moment His body filled the fixed sight on Hawes's gun.

Hawes squeezed the trigger.

There was a mild click, a click that sounded shockingly loud, a click that thundered in Hawes's surprised ears like a cannon explosion.

Smith leaped the airshaft.

Hawes got to his feet, cursing his empty pistol, reloading as he ran across the roof to the airshaft. He looked across it to the next roof. Smith was nowhere in sight. Smith was gone.

Swearing all the way, he headed back for Smith's apartment. There had been no time to reload until it was too late, and once it's too late, there's nothing to be done about it. Walking with his head down, he crossed the sticky tar.

Two shots rang out into the stillness of the summer rooftops, and Hawes hit the tar again. He looked up. A uniformed cop was standing on the edge of the opposite roof ahead, taking careful aim.

"Hold your fire, you dumb bastard!" Hawes yelled. "I'm on your side."

"Throw your gun away," the cop yelled back.

Hawes complied. The cop leaped the airshaft and approached Hawes cautiously. When he saw his face, he said, "Oh, it's you, sir."

"Yes, it's me, sir," Hawes said disgustedly.

The landlady was having none of Cotton Hawes. The landlady was screaming and ranting for him to get out of her building. She had never had trouble with the cops, and now they came around shooting. What was going to happen to her tenants? They'd all move out, all because of him, all because of that big redheaded stupid jerk! Hawes told one of the uniformed cops to keep her downstairs, and then he went into Smith's apartment.

The bed had been slept in the night before. The sheets were still rumpled. Hawes went to the single closet in the bedroom and opened it. There was nothing in the closet except the wire hangers on the rod. Hawes shrugged and went into the bathroom. The sink had been used sometime during that day. Soap was still in the basin, clotted around the drain. He opened the medicine cabinet. A bottle of iodine was on the top shelf. Two bars of soap were on the middle shelf. A pair of scissors, a straight razor, a box of Band-Aids, a tube of shaving cream, a toothbrush, and toothpaste were all crowded onto the lowest shelf. Hawes closed the door, and left the bathroom.

In the bedroom again, he checked through Smith's dresser. *Smith*, he thought, *John Smith*. The phoniest name anybody in the world could pick. The dresser was empty of clothing. In the top drawer, six magazines for an automatic pistol rested in one corner. Hawes lifted one of them with his handkerchief. Unless he was mistaken, the magazine would fit a Luger. He collected the magazines and put them into his pockets.

He went into the kitchen, the sole remaining room in the apartment. A coffee cup was on the kitchen table. A coffeepot was on the stove. Bread crumbs were scattered near the toaster. John Smith had apparently eaten here this morning. Hawes went to the icebox and opened the door.

A loaf of bread and a partially used rectangle of butter were on one of the shelves. That was all.

He opened the ice compartment. A bottle of milk rested alongside a melting cake of ice.

The lab boys would have a lot of work to do in Smith's apartment. But Hawes could do nothing more there at the moment except speculate on the absence of clothing and food, an absence that seemed to indicate that John Smith—whatever his real name was—did not actually live in the apartment. Had he rented the place only to carry out his murder? Had he planned to return here after he'd done his killing? Was he using this as a base of operations? Because it was close to the precinct? Or because it was close to his intended victim? Which?

Hawes closed the door to the ice compartment.

It was then that he heard the sound behind him.

Someone was in the apartment with him.

His gun was in his hand before he whirled.

"Hey!" the woman said. "What's that for?"

Hawes lowered the gun. "Who are you, miss?"

"I live across the hall. The cop downstairs said I should come up here and talk to the detective. Are you the detective?"

"Yes."

"Well, I live across the hall."

The girl was unattractive, a brunette with large brown eyes and very pale skin. She spoke from the side of her mouth, a mannerism that gave her the appearance of a Hollywood gun moll. She was wearing only a thin pink slip, and the one disconcertingly attractive thing about her was the bosom that threatened the silk.

"Did you know this John Smith character?" Hawes asked.

"The few times he was here, I seen him," the girl said. "He only moved in a couple of weeks ago. You know, you noticed him right away."

"How often has he been here since he moved in?"

"Only a couple of times. I came in one night he was here—to introduce myself, you know? Neighborly. What the hell?" The girl shrugged. Her breasts shrugged with her. She was not wearing a brassiere, and Hawes found this disconcerting, too. "He was sitting right there at the kitchen table, cutting up newspapers. I asked him what he was doing. He said he kept a scrapbook."

"When was this?"

"About a week ago."

"He was cutting up newspapers?"

"Yeah," the girl said. "Goofy. Well, he looked goofy, anyway. You know what I mean."

Hawes bent to examine the kitchen table. Studying it closely, he could see traces of paste on the soiled oilcloth covering. Then Smith had composed the letter here, and it had been only a week ago, and not on the Sunday of June 23. He had simply used an old newspaper.

"Was there paste on the table?" Hawes asked her.

"Yeah, I think so. A tube of paste. Well, for his scrapbook, I guess."

"Sure," Hawes said. "Ever talk to him again after that night?"

"Just in the hall."

"How many times?"

"Well, he was here one night after that. Last week, I mean. And then he was here last night."

"Did he sleep here last night?"

"I guess so. How should I know?" The girl seemed suddenly aware that she was wearing only a slip. She crossed one arm over her abundant bosom.

"What time did he get here last night?"

"Pretty late. After midnight, it must've been. I was listening to the radio. It was very hot last night, you know. It's almost impossible to get any sleep in these apartments. They're just like ovens. The door was open, and I heard him down the hall, so I went out to say hello. He was putting the key in the lock, looking just like a Russian spy, I swear to God. All he needed was a bomb, and that would be the picture."

"Did he have anything with him?"

"Just a bag. Groceries, I guess. Oh yeah. Glasses. You know. Opera glasses. I asked him was he just getting back from the opera."

"What did he say?"

"He laughed. He was a hot sketch. Smith. John Smith. That was funny, don't you think?"

"What was funny about it?" Hawes asked.

"Well, the cough drops and all, you know. He was a hot sketch. I guess he won't be coming back after today, huh?"

"I guess not," Hawes said, trying to keep up with the some-what vague conversation.

"Is he a crook or something?"

"We don't know. Did he ever tell you anything about himself?"

"No. Nothing. He didn't talk so much. Anyway, he was only here those few times. And even then, he always seemed in a hurry. I asked him once if this was his summer place. You know, like a joke. He said yeah this was his retreat. A hot sketch. Smith." She laughed at the name.

"But he never told you where he worked. Or even *if* he worked?"

"No." The girl crossed her other arm over her bosom. "I bet-ter go put something on, huh?" she said. "I was taking a little nap when all the shooting started. I got so excited when it was over, I run downstairs in my slip. I'm a real sight, ain't I?" She giggled. "I better go put something on. It was nice talking to you. You don't seem like a bull at all."

"Thank you," Hawes said and then wondered if he was being complimented.

The girl hesitated at the door. "Well, I hope you get him, anyway. He shouldn't be too hard to find. How many like him can there be in the city?"

"How many Smiths, do you mean?" Hawes asked, and the girl thought this was hysterical.

"You're a hot sketch, too," she answered. He watched her as she went down the hall. He shrugged, closed the apartment door behind him, and went downstairs to the street. The landlady was still screaming.

Hawes told one of the patrolmen to keep everybody out of Apartment 22 until the lab boys had gone over it.

Then he went back to the precinct.

It was 5:00 P.M.

Carella was sitting at one of the desks drinking coffee from a container when Hawes walked in. Willis and Meyer had not yet returned. The squadroom was silent

"Hello, Cotton," Carella said.

"Steve," Hawes answered.

"Understand you got into a little fracas on Twelfth?"

"Umm."

"You all right?"

"I'm fine. Except I keep losing people."

"Have some coffee. The desk was really jumping downstairs. Must have got fifty calls about the shooting. He got away again, huh?"

"Umm," Hawes said.

"Well." Carella shrugged. "Cream? Sugar?"

"Little of each."

Carella fixed the coffee and handed the cup to Hawes. "Relax. We can use a rest."

"I want to make a call first."

"Where?"

"Pistol permits." He emptied his pockets onto the desk. "I picked these up in his apartment. Do they look like Luger magazines to you?"

"They damn well couldn't be anything else," Carella said.

"I want to check on permits for Lugers in the precinct Who knows? We may get a break."

"That's the easy way," Carella said. "Nothing ever comes the easy way, Cotton."

"It's worth a try," he said. He looked up at the wall clock. "Jesus," he said. "Five already. Three hours to go."

He pulled the phone to him and made his call. When he'd finished, he picked up the coffee container.

"They'll call me back," he said to Carella. He put his feet up on the desk. "Ahhhhhhhhh."

"Think this damn heat'll ever break?"

"God, I hope so."

In the silence of the squadroom, the two men sipped at their coffee. There was, for the moment, no need for communication. They sat with the afternoon sunlight filtering through the grilled windows, marking the floor with long golden rectangles. They sat with the hum of the electric fans rotating limpid air. They sat with the hushed, faraway street noise below them. They sat, and for the moment they were not policemen working on a difficult case on the hottest day of the year. They were simply two friends having a cup of coffee together.

"I've got a date tonight," Hawes said.

"Nice?" Carella asked.

"A widow," Hawes said. "Very pretty. I met her this afternoon. Or was it this morning? Well, before lunch, anyway. A blonde. Very pretty."

"Teddy's a brunette," Carella said. "Black hair. Very black."

"When do I get to meet her?" Hawes asked.

"I don't know. Name it. I'm supposed to take her to a movie tonight. She's a remarkable lip-reader. She enjoys the movies as much as anyone who can hear."

It no longer surprised Hawes to hear Carella talk about the handicap of his wife, Teddy. She had been born a deaf-mute, but this didn't seem to hinder her in the pursuit of happiness. From what other detectives on the squad had told him, Hawes had pieced together the picture of a lively, interesting, vivacious, and damned beautiful girl, and his mental picture couldn't have been more correct. Too, because he liked Carella, he was predisposed toward liking Teddy, and he really did want to meet her.

"You say you're going to a movie tonight?" Hawes asked.

"Mmm," Carella said.

Hawes balanced the pleasure of meeting Teddy against the pleasure of entertaining Christine Maxwell alone. Christine Maxwell won out, proving the age-old adage, Hawes mused, that gentlemen prefer blondes.

"This is a first date," he said to Carella. "After I get to know her, we'll make it a double, okay?"

"Anytime you say," Carella said.

Again the squadroom fell silent. From the clerical office down the hall, they could hear the steady rat-tat-tat of Miscolo's type-writer. They sat drinking their coffee silently. There was something peaceful about these few minutes of relaxation, these few minutes of suspended time, this breathing spell in the race with the clock.

The moments ended.

"What's this? A country club?" Willis called from the railing.

"Look at them, will ya?" Meyer said. "We're shagging ass all over town, and they're taking their tea and crumpets."

"Blow it out," Carella said.

"How do you like this?" Willis went on, refusing to let it go. "I hear you got shot, Cotton," he said. "The desk sergeant tells me you're a hero."

"No such luck," Hawes replied, regretting the sudden rupture of silence. "He missed."

"Too bad, so sad," Willis said. He was a small detective with the fine-boned body of a jockey. But Fats Donner had told the truth about him; Willis was not a man to fool with. He knew judo the way he knew the penal code, and he could practically break your arm just by looking at you.

Meyer pulled a chair up to the desk. "Hal, go get us some coffee, will you? Miscolo's probably got a pot going."

Willis sighed. "Man, I—"

"Come on, come on," Meyer said. "Respect your elders."

Willis sighed again and departed for the clerical office.

"How'd you make out at the bar, Steve?" Meyer asked.

"Huh?"

"The Pub. Wasn't that the name of it? Anybody make the picture?"

"No. It's a nice bar, though. Right on Thirteenth. Stop in if you're in the neighborhood."

"Did he set up a few for you?" Meyer asked.

"Naturally," Carella said.

"You drunken bastard."

"All I had was two beers."

"That's more than I've had since breakfast," Meyer said. "Where the hell is Willis with that coffee?"

The telephone rang. Hawes picked it up.

"87th Squad, Hawes." He listened. "Oh, hello, Bob. Just a second." He handed the phone to Carella. "It's O'Brien. For you, Steve."

"Hello, Bob," Carella said into the phone.

"Steve, I'm still with this Samalson guy. He just left the supermarket. He's in a bar across the street, tilting one before he heads home, I guess. You still want me to stick with him?"

"Hold on, Bob."

Carella pressed the hold button on the phone and buzzed the lieutenant's office.

"Yes?" Byrnes said.

"I've got O'Brien on the wire," Carella said. "Do you still want that tail on Samalson?"

"Is it eight o'clock yet?" Byrnes asked.

"No."

"Then I still want the tail. Tell Bob to stick with him until he goes to sleep. In fact, I want him watched all night. If he's in this thing, the goddamn shooter may come to him."

"Okay," Carella said, "You going to relieve him later, Pete?"

"Oh, hell, tell him to call me as soon as Samalson gets to the apartment. I'll have a cop from the 102nd relieve him."

"Right," Carella clicked off, pressed the extension button, and said, "Bob, stick with him until he's in his apartment. Then call Pete, and he'll get somebody from the 102nd to spell you. He wants this to be an all-night plant."

"Suppose he doesn't head home?" O'Brien asked.

"What can I tell you, Bob?"

"Shit! I'm supposed to go to a ball game tonight."

"I'm supposed to go to a movie. Look, this thing'll be over by eight."

"It'll be over for the shooter, sure. But Pete figures he may be tied in with Samalson, doesn't he?"

"He doesn't really believe that, Bob. But he's trying to cover every angle. Samalson's story was a little thin."

"You think the killer's going to seek a guy who's already been interrogated by the cops? That's faulty reasoning, Steve."

"It's a hot day, Bob. Maybe all of Pete's cylinders aren't clicking."

"Sure, but where does—oh, oh, the bastard's on his way. I'll call in a little later. Listen, do me a favor, will you?"

"What's that?"

"Crack this by eight. I want to see that ball game."

"We'll try."

"He's moving. So long, Steve." O'Brien hung up.

"O'Brien," Carella said. "He's beefing about the tail on Samalson. Thinks it's ridiculous. I think so, too. Samalson didn't have the smell on him."

"What smell?" Meyer asked.

"You know the smell. Every thief in the city gives it off. Samalson didn't have it. If he's tied in with this, I'll eat his goddamn field glasses."

The phone rang again.

"That's probably Samalson," Hawes said, "complaining about O'Brien tailing him."

Smiling, Carella picked up the receiver. "87th Squad, Detective Carella," he said. "Oh, sure." He covered the mouthpiece. "Permits. You want me to take it down?"

"Go ahead."

"Shoot," Carella said to the mouthpiece. He listened for a moment, then turned to Hawes. "Forty-seven registered Lugers in the precinct. You want them all?"

"I just thought of something," Hawes said.

"What?"

"They take your fingerprints for the back of a pistol-license application. If—"

"Never mind," Carella said into the phone. "Forget it. Thanks a lot." He hung up. "If our boy," he concluded for Hawes, "had a permit, the fingerprints would be on file at the IB. *Ergo*, our boy ain't got a permit."

Hawes nodded. "You ever have a day like that, Steve?"

"Like what?"

"Where you're just plain stupid," Hawes said despondently.

"I knew you were calling Permits, didn't I?" Carella asked. "Did I try to stop you?"

Hawes sighed and stared through the window. Willis came back with the coffee.

"Here you are, sir," he said to Meyer. "I hope everything is satisfactory, sir."

"I'll leave a big tip," Meyer said, and he picked up the coffee cup and then cleared his throat.

"I've got a tip for you," Willis said.

"What's that?"

"Never become a cop. The hours are long, and the pay is low, and you have to do all sorts of menial chores for your colleagues."

"I'm getting a cold," Meyer said. He reached into his back pocket and pulled out a box of cough drops. "I always get summer colds. They're the worst kind, and I always get them." He put a cough drop on his tongue. "Anybody want one of these?"

Nobody answered. Meyer returned the box to his back pocket. He picked up his coffee and began sipping at it.

"Quiet," Willis said.

"Yeah."

"You think it really is a *specific* lady?" Hawes asked.

"I don't know," Carella said. "But I think so, yes."

"He used the name John Smith," Hawes said. "When he moved into this apartment. No clothes there. No food."

"John Smith. *Cherchez la femme,*" Meyer said. "*Cherchez* Pocohontas.*"

"We've been *cherchez*-ing *la femme* all day," Hawes said. "I'm getting weary."

"Stick it out, kid," Carella said. He looked up at the wall clock. "It's five-fifteen. It'll all be over soon."

And then it started.

It started with the fat woman in the housedress, and her arrival at the slatted-rail divider seemed to trip off a train of events, none of which had any immediate bearing on the case. It was terribly unfortunate that the events intruded upon the smooth progress of the investigation. None of the 87th's cops would have had it that way if there had been a choice. They were, after all, rather intent upon preventing a murder that night. But the men of the 87th were working stiffs doing a job, and the things that happened within the next fifty minutes were not things that fit into place like the pieces of a jigsaw puzzle. They followed no pat line of development. They brought the cops not an iota closer to finding The Lady or the man who had threatened to kill. The train of events started at 5:15 in the late afternoon of Wednesday, July 24. They did not end until 6:05 P.M. in the evening of that same day.

All they did was consume the most valuable commodity the detectives had: time.

The woman in the housedress puffed up to the slatted-rail divider. She was holding the hand of a ten-year-old blond kid in dungarees and a red-striped T-shirt. The kid was Frankie Annuci. The woman was controlling a rage that threatened to burst her seams. Her face was livid, her eyes were sparkling black coals, her lips were compressed tightly into a narrow line that held back the flow of her anger. She charged up to the railing as if she would batter it down by sheer momentum and then stopped abruptly. The steam building inside her pushed past the thin retaining line of her lips. Her mouth opened. The words came out in a roar.

"WHERE'S THE LIEUTENANT HERE?"

Meyer almost spilled his coffee and swallowed his cough drop. He whirled around in his chair. Willis, Carella, and Hawes stared at the woman as if she were the Ghost of Criminals Past.

"THE LIEUTENANT!" she shouted. "THE LIEUTENANT! Where is he?"

Carella rose and walked to the railing. He spotted the boy and said, "Hello, Frankie. What can I do for you, ma'am? Is there—"

"Don't say hello to him!" the woman shouted. "Don't even look at him! Who are you?"

"Detective Carella."

"Well, Detective Carella, I want to talk…" She stopped. "*Tu sei 'taliano?*"

"*Si,*" Carella said.

"*Bene. Dove il tenente? Voglio parlare con—*"

"I don't understand Italian too well," Carella said.

"You don't? Why not? Where's the lieutenant?"

"Well, can I help you?"

"Did you have Frankie in here this afternoon?"

"Yes."

"Why?"

"To ask him some questions."

"I'm his mother. I'm Mrs. Annuci. Mrs. Rudolph Annuci. I'm a good woman, and my husband is a good man. Why did you have my son in here?"

"He delivered a letter for somebody this morning, Mrs. Annuci. We're looking for the man who gave him the letter, that's all. We just asked him some questions.

"YOU HAD NO RIGHT TO DO THAT!" Mrs. Annuci shouted. "HE IS NOT A CRIMINAL!"

"Nobody said he was," Carella answered.

"THEN, WHAT WAS HE DOING IN A POLICE STATION!"

"I just told you..."

A phone began ringing somewhere in the squadroom. It synchronized with what Mrs. Annuci screamed next so that all Carella heard was:

"WELL I WAS NEVERRRRRING SO EMBRRRRRRING IN MY LIFE!"

"Now, now, *signora*," Carella said.

Meyer picked up the phone. "87th Squad, Detective Meyer."

"Don't *signora* me, I'm not your old grandmother! Humiliated! Humiliated! *Vergogna, vergogna!* He was picked up by one of the Snow Whites. Right in the street! Standing with a bunch of boys, and the Snow White pulls to the curb and two cops get out and grab him. Like—"

"What?" Meyer said.

Mrs. Annuci turned to him. "I said two cops—" and then she saw he was talking to the phone.

"Okay, we'll move!" Meyer said. He hung up rapidly. "Willis, come on! Holdup in progress on Tenth and Culver. The guy's shooting it out with the beat cop and two squad cars!"

"Holy Jesus!" Willis said.

They ran through the gate in the railing, nearly knocking Mrs. Annuci down.

"Criminals!" she said as they rushed down the stairs. "You deal with criminals. You take my son into the police station, and you mix him with thieves. He's a good boy, a boy who—" She stopped suddenly. "Did you beat him? Did you use a hose on him?"

"No, no, of course not, Mrs. Annuci," Carella said, and then he was distracted by a sound on the metal steps outside. A man in handcuffs appeared at the top of the steps, and then another man stumbled in behind him, his face oozing blood. Mrs. Annuci turned, following Carella's gaze, just as the patrolman came into view behind the pair. The patrolman shoved at the man with the handcuffs. Mrs. Annuci gasped.

"Oh, my God!" she said. "Jesus, Mary, and Joseph!"

Hawes was already on his feet, walking toward the railing.

"Mrs. Annuci," Carella was saying, "why don't we sit down here on the bench where we can—"

"What've you got?" Hawes asked the patrolman.

"His head! Look at his head!" Mrs. Annuci said, her face going white. "Don't look, Frankie," she added, contradicting herself.

The man's head was indeed a sorry-looking mess. The hair was matted with blood, which trickled onto his face and neck, staining his white T-shirt. There was an open cut on his forehead, too, and the cut streamed blood onto the bridge of his nose.

"This son of a bitch used a baseball bat on him, sir," the patrolman said. "The guy bleeding is a pusher. Desk lieutenant thought there might be a dope angle to this, figured you should question him."

"I ain't no pusher," the bleeding man said. "I want him sent to prison! He hit me with a bat!"

"You'd better get him to a hospital," Hawes said, looking at the bleeding man.

"No hospital! Not until he's in prison! He hit me with a ball bat! This son of a bitch—"

"Ohhhh," Mrs. Annuci said.

"Come on outside," Carella said. "We'll sit on that bench, all right? I'll explain everything that happened with your son."

Hawes pulled the man with the handcuffs into the room. "Get in there!" he said. "Take off the cuffs, Alec," he said to the patrol-man. "You better get to the hospital, mister," he said to the bleed-ing man.

"No hospital!" the man insisted. "Not until he's booked and sent to jail."

The patrolman took the cuffs off the other man.

"Get some wet rags for this guy's head," Hawes said, and the patrolman left. "What's your name, mister?"

"Mendez," the bleeder said. "Raoul Mendez."

"And you're no pusher, huh, Raoul?"

"I never pushed junk in my life. That's a crock, believe me. This guy just came over—"

Hawes turned to the other man. "What's your name?"

"—you!" the man said.

Hawes looked at him steadily.

"Empty your pockets on that desk."

The man did not move.

"I said—"

The man suddenly lunged at Hawes, his fists swinging wildly. Hawes clamped one hand into the man's shirt collar and rammed the other clenched fist into his face. The man staggered back sev-eral paces, bunched his fists again, and came at Hawes once more. Hawes chopped a quick right to his gut, and the man doubled over.

"Empty your pockets, punk," Hawes said tightly.

The man emptied his pockets.

"Now. What's your name?" Hawes asked as he went through the accumulation that had been in the man's trousers.

"John Begley. You hit me again, you son of a bitch, and I'll—"

"Shut your mouth!" Hawes snapped.

Begley shut up instantly.

"Why'd you go at him with a ball bat?"

"That's my business," Begley said.

"It's mine, too," Hawes answered.

"He tried to kill me," Mendez said. "Assault! First-degree assault! That's Section 240. Assault with intent to kill!"

"I didn't try to kill him," Begley said. "If I wanted to kill him, he wouldn't be walking around right now!"

"You're familiar with the penal law, huh, Mendez?" Hawes asked.

"I hear guys talking about it in the neighborhood," Mendez said. "Hell, everybody knows Section 240. Assault is common."

"240's first-degree assault, Begley," Hawes said. "You can get ten years for that. 242 is assault in the second degree. No more than five years and a fine, maybe just the fine. Which are you trying for?"

"I didn't try to kill him."

"Is he a pusher?"

"Ask him."

"I'm asking you."

"I'm no stoolie. I don't know what the hell he is. I didn't try to kill him. I just wanted to bust a couple of arms and legs. Legs, especially."

"Why?"

"He's been chasing my wife."

"What do you mean?"

"What the hell do you think I mean?"

"How about that, Mendez?"

"He's crazy. I don't even know his wife."

"You lying son of a bitch!" Begley said, and he started for Mendez.

Hawes shoved him away. "Cool off, Begley, or I'll knock you on your ass!"

"He knows my wife!" Begley shouted. "He knows her too goddamn good! I'll get that bastard! If I go to jail, I'll get him when I get out!"

"He's crazy, I told you!" Mendez said. "Crazy! I was standing on the corner minding my own business, and he came up with the ball bat and started swinging."

"All right, all right, keep quiet," Hawes said.

The patrolman came back with the wet cloths.

"We won't need those, Alec," Hawes said. "Get this man to a hospital before he bleeds to death right here in the squadroom."

"Not until *he* goes to prison!" Mendez shouted. "I ain't leav—"

"You want to go to prison yourself, Mendez?" Hawes said. "For resisting an officer?"

"Who's—"

"Get the hell out of here! Your pusher smell is stinking up the squadroom!"

"I'm no pusher!"

"He's a pusher, sir," the patrolman said. "He's been put away twice already."

"Get the hell out, Mendez," Hawes said.

"A pusher? You got me wrong—"

"And if I ever catch you with any junk on you, I'll take a ball bat to you myself! Now clear out! Get him to the hospital, Alec."

"Come on," the patrolman said, taking Mendez's arm.

"A pusher," Mendez mumbled, as they went through the railing. "Man, a guy takes one fall, right away he's labeled."

"*Two* falls," the patrolman corrected.

"Okay, two, two," Mendez said as they went down the steps.

Mrs. Annuci swallowed.

"So you see," Carella said to her, "all we did was ask some questions. Your son is something of a hero, Mrs. Annuci. You can tell that to your neighbors."

"And have this killer come after him next? No, thank you, no, thank you."

In the squadroom, Hawes said, "Were you trying to kill him, Begley?"

"I told you. No. Look—"

"What?"

Begley's voice trailed to a whisper. "This is only second-degree assault. The guy was making it with my wife. I mean, what the hell, suppose it was your wife?"

"I'm not married."

"Okay, but suppose. You going to send me to jail for protecting my home?"

"That's up to the judge," Hawes said.

Begley's voice went even lower. "Let's judge it ourselves, huh?"

"What?"

"What'll it cost? Three bills? Half a century?"

"You've got the wrong cop," Hawes said.

"Come on, come on," Begley said, smiling.

Hawes picked up the phone and buzzed the desk. Artie Knowles, the sergeant who'd relieved Murchison at 4:00 P.M., answered.

"Artie, this is Cotton Hawes. You can book this bum. Make it second-degree assault. Send somebody up for him, will you?"

"Right!" Knowles said.

"You kidding?" Begley asked.

"I'm serious," Hawes said.

"You're turning down five hundred bucks?"

"Are you offering it? We can add that to the charge."

"Never mind, never mind," Begley said hastily. "I ain't offering nothing. Boy!"

He was still "Boy"-ing when the patrolman led him downstairs, passing Bert Kling in the hallway. Kling was a tall and youthful blond detective. He was wearing a leather jacket and dungarees. His denim shirt under the jacket was stained with sweat.

"Hi," he said to Hawes. "What's up?"

"Assault," Hawes said. "You finished for the day?"

"Yeah," Kling said. "This waterfront plant is for the birds. I'll never learn anything. There isn't a guy on the docks who doesn't know I'm a cop."

"Have they really tipped to you?"

"I guess not, but nobody's talking about heroin, that's for sure. Why the hell doesn't Pete leave this to the Narcotics Squad?"

"He's trying to get a jump on the precinct pushers. Wants to know where the stuff's coming in. You know how Pete feels about dope."

"Whose hand is Steve holding, outside?"

"Hysterical mother," Hawes said, and then he heard Meyer's voice coming up the stairway. Kling took off his jacket.

"Brother, I'm hot," he said. "You ever try unloading a ship?"

"Nope," Hawes said.

"Get in there, you rotten hood," Meyer said, "and don't give me any back talk." He glanced at the woman on the bench only cursorily and then shoved at his prisoner. The man he shoved was wearing handcuffs. The cuffs were tight on his wrists.

A pair of police handcuffs resembles the five-and-dime stuff purchased for kids, except the police stuff is for real. They are made out of steel, forged into a slender, narrow, impervious, portable jail. The movable arm is bolted into the body of the cuff. The movable arm has a sawtooth edge that, when engaged with the body, catches and holds there. Like blood traveling through a vein, the sawtooth edge cannot reverse its course; it can only move forward. It can, in fact, move completely through the body of the cuff itself, completing a full circle, so that a key is not necessary to open the wristlet before it is clamped onto the wrist. The arresting officer simply squeezes the movable arm into and through the body of the cuff until the arm emerges on the other side. He then clamps it onto the wrist and wedges it shut again. The wrist prevents the movable arm from making the full circle again. To take the cuff off the wrist, a key is necessary.

A trio of metal links attaches one wrist cuff to the other. The cuffs are not at all comfortable. If they are placed on the wrists with care, it is possible to keep them from biting into the flesh. But the average arresting officer squeezes the cuff to snap the movable arm into its open position and then hastily clamps the cuff onto the wrist and squeezes again until the metal collides with flesh and bone. When a pair of handcuffs is taken off a prisoner, the prisoner's wrists are usually raw and lacerated—and sometimes bleeding.

Not very much delicacy had been used on the man Meyer led into the squadroom. He had just been shooting it out with a gang of policemen, and when they had finally collared him, they'd clamped the cuffs onto his wrists with barely controlled ferocity. The metal was biting into his flesh and paining him. Meyer shoved him into the room, and the metal cuffs bit further as he moved his arms trying to maintain his balance.

"Here's a big man," Meyer said to Hawes. "Tried to hold off half the precinct, didn't you, big man?"

The prisoner did not answer.

"The jewelry store on Tenth and Culver," Meyer said. "He was inside with a gun when the beat patrolman spotted him. Brave man. A daylight holdup. You're a brave man, aren't you?"

The prisoner did not answer.

"He started shooting the minute he saw the patrolman. A cruising squad car heard the shots and joined the battle, and then radioed for another car. The second car called back here for help. A regular hero's siege, huh, big man?" Meyer asked.

The prisoner did not answer.

"Sit down, big man," Meyer said.

The prisoner sat.

"What's your name?"

"Louis Gallagher."

"You been in trouble before, Gallagher?"

"No."

"We'll check it, so don't start with a snow job."

"I've never been in trouble before," Gallagher said.

"Miscolo got any coffee?" Kling asked, and he started down the corridor. Carella was just returning from the steps. "Get rid of her, Steve?"

"Yeah," Carella said. "How were the docks?"

"Hot."

"You plan on going home?"

"Yeah. Soon as I have some coffee."

"You'd better stick around. We've got a nut loose."

"What do you mean?"

"A letter. Going to kill a dame at eight tonight. Stick around. Pete may need you."

"I'm bushed, Steve."

"No kidding?" Carella said, and he walked into the squadroom.

"You've got a record, haven't you, Gallagher?" Meyer asked.

"No. I told you once already."

"Gallagher, we've got a lot of unsolved holdups in this neighborhood."

"That's your problem. You're the cops."

"You do them?"

"I held up the store today because I need dough. That's all. This is the first time I ever did anything like this. How about taking the cuffs off and letting me go?"

"Oh, brother, you slay me," Willis said. He turned to Hawes. "He tries to shoot us, and then he cops a plea."

"Who's copping a plea?" Gallagher said. "I'm asking you to forget the whole thing."

Willis stared at the man as if he were a dangerous lunatic ready to begin slashing passersby with a razor. "It must be the heat," he said unblinkingly.

"Come on," Gallagher said. "How about it? How about giving me a break?"

"Look—"

"What the hell did I do? Shoot a little? Did I hurt anybody? Hell, I gave you a little excitement. Come on, be good guys. Take off these cuffs and send me on my way."

Willis mopped his brow. "He isn't kidding, you know that, don't you, Meyer?"

"Come on, Meyer," Gallagher said, "be a sp—" and Meyer slapped him across the face.

"Don't talk to me, big man. Don't use my name, or I'll ram it down your throat. This your first holdup?"

Gallagher looked at Meyer with hooded eyes, nursing his hurt cheek. "You I wouldn't give the sweat off my—" he started, and Meyer hit him again.

"How many other holdups you pull in this precinct?"

Gallagher was silent.

"Somebody asked you a question, Gallagher," Willis said.

Gallagher looked up at Willis, including him in his hatred.

Carella walked over to the group. "Well, well, hello, Louie," he said.

Gallagher looked at him blankly. "I don't know you," he said.

"Why, Louie," Carella said, "your memory is getting bad. Don't you remember me? Steve Carella. Think, Louie."

"Is this guy a bull?" Gallagher asked. "I never seen him before in my life."

"The bakery, Louie? 1949? South Third? Remember, Louie?"

"I don't eat cake," Gallagher said.

"You weren't there buying cake, Louie. You were sticking up the joint. I happened to be walking by. Remember now?"

"Oh," Gallagher said. "That."

"When'd you get out, Louie?" Carella asked.

"What difference does it make? I'm out."

"And back at the old pushcart," Meyer said. "When'd you get out?"

"You got ten years for armed robbery, Gallagher," Carella said. "What happened? Parole?"

"Yeah."

"When did you get out?" Meyer repeated.

"About six months ago," Gallagher said.

"I guess you enjoyed your stay with the state, huh?" Meyer asked. "You're itching to get back."

"Come on, let's forget the whole deal," Gallagher said. "Whattya wanna be rotten guys for, huh?"

"Why do *you* want to be a rotten guy, Gallagher?"

"Who, me? I don't want to be rotten," Gallagher said. "It's a compulsion."

"Now I've seen everything," Meyer said. "Psychiatrist thieves! It's too much, too much. Come on, bum, the lieutenant's gonna want to talk to you. On your feet. Come on."

One of the phones rang. Hawes picked it up.

"87th Squad, Hawes," he said.

"Cotton, this is Sam Grossman."

"Hello, Sam, what've you got?"

"Nothing much. Prints that match up with the ones on the glasses, but...Well, let's face it, Cotton. We haven't got time to give that apartment the going-over it should get. Not before eight o'clock, anyway."

"Why? What time is it?" Hawes asked.

"It's past six already," Grossman said, and Hawes looked up at the wall clock and saw that it was exactly five minutes past six. Where had the last hour gone?

"Yeah. Well..." he started, and then he couldn't think of anything to say.

"There's just one thing that might help you," Grossman said. "Maybe you saw it already."

"What's that?"

"We picked it up in the kitchen. On the windowsill over the sink. It has the suspect's prints on it, so maybe he used it. In any case, he handled it."

"What, Sam?"

"A card. You know, a business card."

"What's the business?" Hawes asked, picking up a pencil.

"It's a card for the Jo-George Diner. That's two words, hyphenated. No e on the Jo."

"Address?"

"336 North 13th."

"Anything else on the card?"

"Right-hand corner of the card says, 'Fine Food.' That's it."

"Thanks, Sam. I'll get right over there."

"Sure. Maybe the suspect eats there, who knows? Or maybe he's one of the owners."

"Jo or George, huh?"

"It could be," Grossman said. "You don't figure this joker lived in that apartment, do you?"

"No. Do you?"

"A few signs of habitation, but all recent. Nothing prolonged. My guess is that he used it as a pied-à-terre, if you'll pardon the Japanese."

"That's what I figure, too," Hawes said quickly. "Sam, I'd love to throw the bull with you, but it's getting late. I'd better hit that diner."

"Go ahead," Grossman said. "Good luck."

The Jo-George Diner was on The Stem at Thirteenth Street. Because the diner's entrance was on the side street rather than the avenue, the address was 336 North 13th. There were no trucks parked outside it, but Hawes formed no opinions about the quality of the food. Perhaps trucks would have been there were there not parking regulations against them.

The diner looked like any other diner in the city, or perhaps even every other diner in the world. Metallically glistening in the sun still lingering in the sky, it squatted on the corner, a large sign across its top announcing the name JO-GEORGE DINER.

It was 6:15 P.M. when Hawes climbed the steps and opened the front door. The diner was packed.

The jukebox was blaring, and there was the persistent hum of conversation bouncing off the walls and the ceiling. There were several waitresses scurrying back and forth between the booths and the counter. Two men were behind the counter, and Hawes could see beyond the pass-through into the kitchen, where three more men worked. The Jo-George Diner was a thriving little spot, and Hawes wondered which of the men were the owners.

He looked for a stool at the counter, but they were all occupied. He went to stand alongside the cash register at one end of the counter. The waitresses scurried past, ignoring him, picking up their orders. The men behind the counter dashed from customer to customer.

"Hey!" Hawes said.

One of the men stopped. "There'll be a short wait, sir," he said. "If you'll just stand over there near the cigarette machine, away from the door, somebody'll get up and you—"

"Jo around?" Hawes asked.

"It's his day off," the man said. "You a friend of—"

"George here?"

The man looked puzzled. He was a man in his late fifties with iron-gray hair and blue eyes. He was heavily built, his shirtsleeves rolled up over muscular biceps. "*I'm* George," he said. "Who are you?"

"Detective Hawes. 87th Squad. Is there anyplace we can talk, Mr....?" He let the sentence trail.

"Laddona," George said. "George Laddona. What's this about?"

"Just a few questions, that's all."

"What about?"

"Can we talk someplace besides here?"

"You sure picked a hell of a time. I got my big supper crowd here right now. Can't you come back later?"

"This can't wait," Hawes said.

"We can talk in the kitchen, I guess."

Hawes listened to the sounds emanating from the bustling kitchen, the orders being shouted, the pots and pans being thrown around, the dishes being washed.

"Anyplace quieter?"

"The only other place is the men's room. It's okay with me if it's okay with you."

"Fine," Hawes said.

George came from behind the counter, and they walked to the other end of the diner. They opened a door that had no lettering on it, just the figure of a man in a top hat. The ladies' room featured a woman with a parasol. When they were inside, Hawes locked the door.

"What's your partner's name?" he asked.

"Jo Cort. Why?"

"Is that his full name?"

"Sure."

"The Jo, I mean."

"Sure. Jo. J-o. Why?"

Hawes pulled the police drawing out of his pocket. He unfolded it and showed it to George.

"This your partner?"

George looked at the picture. "Nope," he said.

"You sure?"

"Don't I know my own partner?"

"Ever see this man in the diner before?"

George shrugged. "Who knows? You know how many people I get in here? Take a look outside. That's how busy it is every night at this time. Who recognizes individuals?"

"Take another look," Hawes said. "He may be a regular."

George looked at the picture again. "There's something familiar about the eyes," he said. He looked at it more closely. "Funny, I..." He shrugged. "No. No, I don't place him, I'm sorry."

Disappointedly, Hawes folded the picture and returned it to his pocket. The card looked like another false lead. The picture was certainly not a drawing of George, and George had just now said it wasn't his partner, either. Where did he go now? What did he ask next? What time was it? How long before the bullet from a Luger crashed into the body of an unsuspecting woman? Was a cop with the prostitute known as 'The Lady'? Did Jay Astor have her police protection yet? Had Philip Bannister left to meet his mother at the ballet? Where was John Smith now? Who was John Smith? What do I ask now?

He pulled the business card from his wallet.

"Recognize this, George?" he asked.

George took the card. "Sure. That's our card."

"You carry them?"

"Sure."

"Jo carry them?"

"Sure. Also, we leave them on the counter. There's a little box for them. People pick them up all the time. Word-of-mouth advertising. It works, believe me. You saw how packed it was out there." He seemed to suddenly remember his customers. "Look, is this going to take much longer? I got to get back."

"Tell me about your setup here," Hawes said, unwilling to leave just yet, unwilling to let go of a lead that had taken him here to this diner, a card found in the apartment of the man who'd called himself John Smith, a man who was not George Laddona and not Jo Cort, but where had the man got the card? Had he eaten here? Hadn't George said there was something familiar about the eyes? Could the man have eaten here? *Dammit, where was he? Who was he? I'm losing my grip*, Hawes thought.

"Regular partnership setup," George said, shrugging. "It's the same all over. Jo and me are partners."

"How old is Jo?"

"Thirty-four."

"And you?"

"Fixty-six."

"That's a big difference. Know him long?"

"About eleven years," George said.

"You get along with him?"

"Fine."

"How'd you meet?"

"At the 52-20 Club. You were in the service, weren't you?"

"Sure."

"Remember when you got out, they had this thing where the state gave you twenty bucks a week for a maximum of fifty-two weeks. A sort of rehabilitation thing. Until you found work."

"I remember," Hawes said. "But you weren't in the service, were you?"

"No, no, I was too old."

"Was Jo?"

"He was 4-F during the war. Had a punctured eardrum or something."

"Then how'd you meet at the 52—"

"We were both working there. For the Welfare Board, you know. Jo and me. That's how we met."

"What happened then?"

"Well, you know, we got friendly. I'd trust him with my right arm. Straight from the beginning. It was just one of those friendships. You know, we hit it off right away. It started with us stopping for a few brews on the way home from work. We still do it. Whenever we work together, we stop for a few brews. Place down the street. Jo and me, the guzzlers." George smiled. "The guzzlers," he repeated fondly.

"Go ahead," Hawes said. He looked at his wristwatch. He had the oddest feeling that he was wasting precious time listening to this fraternal account. "Go ahead," he said again, more impatiently this time.

"Well, we got to discussing our dreams and ambitions. I had a little dough socked away, and so did Jo. We talked about opening a little business. First we thought we'd open a bar, but it costs a lot of money to equip one, you know, and then there's the liquor license and all. We just didn't have that kind of dough."

"So you decided on a diner instead."

"Yeah. We got a loan from the bank, and together with what we had, that was enough to start the business. Partners. Me and Jo. Fifty-fifty split. And it works, believe me. You know why?"

"Why?"

"Because we've got ambition. Both of us. Ambition to get ahead, to make something of ourselves. In a few years we'll be opening another diner, and then later on another. Ambition. And trust." George's voice dropped to a more confidential tone. "Listen, I trust that kid...I trust him like he was my own son." He began chuckling. "Hell, you have to, in my position."

"What do you mean?"

"I'm an orphan, all alone in the world. Jo's the only one I've got. And this is a partnership. That kid's as good as gold. I wouldn't trade him for the world."

"Where is he today?" Hawes asked.

"Wednesday. His day off. We both work Saturdays and Sundays, and we each take a day during the week. We're building, you know. Toward the big string of diners." George smiled.

"You think Jo might have given your card to the man whose picture I showed you?"

"He might have. Why don't you show him the picture?"

"Where can I reach him?"

"I'll give you his phone number. You can call him at home. If he's not there, he's probably with his girlfriend. A nice girl. Her name's Felicia. He'll probably marry her someday."

"Where does he live?" Hawes asked.

"In a nice apartment downtown. One of these hotel apartments. Very nice. He likes to live nice. Me, any hole in the wall'll do. But not Jo. He's…You know, a smart kid. Likes nice things."

"Give me the number," Hawes said.

"You can make the call right here, in the kitchen. There's a phone on the wall. Listen, can we get out of here? Besides my customers, it's getting hot as hell in this cubbyhole."

He opened the door, and they started walking toward the kitchen.

"It's like this every night," George said. "Jam-packed. We give them quality, and it pays off for us. But, boy, it's a lot of work. This won't begin slacking off until seven-thirty, eight o'clock. Busy. Busy all the time. Knock wood," he added, rapping on the counter.

Hawes followed him back to the kitchen. The kitchen was very hot, hot with the heat of the day and the heat of the stoves, and hot with hurried, frantic speech.

"Phone's over there," George said. "The number's Delville 2-4523."

"Thanks," Hawes said,

He walked to the phone and deposited a dime. Then he began dialing. He waited.

"Riverdix Hotel," the voice said.

"Jo Cort, please," Hawes said.

"I'll try his apartment, sir. One moment, please."

Hawes waited. The operator rang.

"I'm sorry, sir. He doesn't seem to be answering."

"Try it again," Hawes said.

"Yes, sir." She tried it again. And again. And again and again. "I'm sorry, sir," she told him. "There's still no answer."

"Thank you," Hawes said, and he hung up.

He went out front and found George.

"He's not home."

"Oh. Too bad. Try his girlfriend. Felicia Pannet. She's in Isola, too."

"Where?" Hawes asked.

"I don't know the address. Midtown someplace. Or just above the Square, I think. Yeah, that's it. On the north side." George turned to a customer. "Yes, sir," he said, "would you care to see a menu?"

"Just give me a bacon and tomato on toast," the man said. "And a cup of coffee."

George turned to the pass-through leading to the kitchen. "BT down," he shouted. "Draw one!" He turned back to Hawes. "Will I be glad when *this* day is over. Know what I'm going to do?"

"What?" Hawes said.

"As soon as this crowd thins out, half hour or so from now, I'm going for a brew. Right down the street. Maybe two brews. Maybe I'll sit there and drink all night. I'm so thirsty I could drink a keg of the stuff. I can't wait. Half hour or so, *whizzz*, I'm out of here."

He had mentioned time, the enemy, and so Hawes unconsciously looked at his wristwatch. It was three minutes to seven.

An hour to go.

"Thanks," he said to George, and he left the diner.

Outside, he wondered what to do. The girl lived in midtown Isola, above the Square. Should he go there? Was it worth it? Suppose Jo wasn't there? Or suppose he *was* there and couldn't identify the picture? Or suppose he *could* identify the picture, would there be time to stop the killer? He looked at his watch again.

7:00.

Was there time?

Could they stop him now? Could they stop him from killing the woman, whoever she was?

Well, what else was there to do? Go back to the precinct squadroom and wait for the hour to pass? Sit there with the boys while a killer took aim at his target, while a Luger was brought to bear and then fired?

What the hell else was there to do? If he hurried, if he put on the siren and cleared the streets, he could be there in ten minutes. Another ten to talk to Jo—if he was there—and then ten to get back to the precinct. He could be in the squadroom by 7:30, and maybe Jo *would* identify that picture. Maybe, maybe, *maybe...*

Hawes walked into a drugstore and directly to the phone booths. He looked up Felicia Pannet's address, got it, and then decided to call her first. If Jo Cort wasn't there, she would tell him so and save him a trip.

He repeated the number to himself, went into the booth, and dialed it.

The busy signal clicked in his ear.

He hung up and waited. Then he dialed again.

Still busy.

Dammit, he was wasting time. If the phone was busy, *some-body* was home! And he sure as hell couldn't spend the next precious hour in a phone booth. He left the drugstore and walked back to the police sedan.

He gunned away from the curb and turned on the siren.

Nathan Hale Square divided the island of Isola almost exactly in two. Dominated by the huge statue of the patriot, it was the hub of a bigger square of city commerce. Swank shops, bookshops, drugstores, automobile showrooms, hotels, and the new giant sports arena surrounded the square with their bustling activity. The heat had in no way diminished the bustle or the hustle accompanying it. The heat very rarely affects pursuit of the long green.

And yet, seeming to typify a more gracious bygone time when the only thing people had to worry about was revolutions, Nathan Hale complacently looked out at the commercialism surrounding him, seemed in fact to look above and beyond it. And like dutiful subjects, a smattering of citizens sat on the benches circling the statue, feeding the pigeons, or reading newspapers, or just watching the girls in their thin summer frocks go by. Watching the girls in their summer frocks was a favorite city pastime and another thing the heat could not affect.

Stopped for a moment by the maze of traffic in the square, Hawes watched the girls in their thin dresses. The traffic broke, the siren erupted, the car gunned forward, the girls were behind him. He swung around the square, heard a motorist curse behind him, and then headed east, taking the corner into Felicia Pannet's block on two wheels. He pulled the sedan to the curb, yanked the keys from the ignition, slammed out of the car, and took the front-stoop steps two at a time to the entrance lobby.

Felicia Pannet, the card in the bell panel read. Hawes pushed the button. He waited, his hand on the knob of the inner door. The door clicked; the lock sprang. Hawes pushed open the door and stepped into the ground-floor lobby. An elevator was at the rear of the lobby. He started for it, then remembered he hadn't looked at Felicia's apartment number. Cursing, muttering proverbs about haste making waste, he went back to the entrance door, opened it, braced it with one foot, and leaned into the lobby to read the apartment number in the bell panel. 63.

He went back inside to the elevator, pushed the *down* button and waited. The indicator told him the elevator was on the seventh floor. He waited. Either the indicator was broken or the elevator was not moving. He pushed the button again. The elevator stayed on the seventh floor.

He could visualize two fat matrons discussing their arthritis, one of them holding the elevator door open while the second fumbled for her apartment keys in her purse. Or perhaps a delivery boy shuttling a month's supply of groceries from the elevator to some apartment, having wedged the door open with the shopping cart. He pushed the button again. Adamantly, the damned elevator refused to move. Hawes looked at his watch and then took the steps.

He was winded and dripping wet when he reached the sixth floor. He looked for Apartment 63, found it, and pushed the black buzzer button in the doorjamb. No one answered. He pushed it again. As he was pushing it, he heard the hum of the elevator, saw the lighted car pass on its way downward to the street.

"Who is it?" a voice from within the apartment asked. The voice was low and cool, a woman's voice.

"Police," Hawes said.

Footsteps padded toward the door. The peephole flap grated metal against metal when it swung back. The peephole presented only a mirrored surface to whoever was standing outside the doorway. The woman inside could see out, but Hawes could not see in.

"I'm not dressed," the voice said. "You'll have to wait."

"Please hurry," Hawes said.

"I'll dress as quickly as I know how," the voice said, and Hawes felt he had been reprimanded. The peephole flap grated shut again. Hawes leaned against the wall opposite the doorway, waiting. It was hot in the corridor. The collected smells of the day had merged with the cooking smells of the evening, and these, in turn, had merged with the heat to form an assault wave on the nostrils. He pulled out his handkerchief and blew his nose. It didn't help.

He realized all at once that he was hungry. He had not eaten since noontime, and he'd done a lot of chasing around since then, and his stomach was beginning to growl.

It'll soon be over, he thought, one way or the other. Then you can go home and shave and put on a clean white shirt and a tie and the gray tropical, and you can pick up Christine Maxwell. You didn't promise her dinner, but you'll buy her dinner, anyway. You'll have some long, tall drinks rammed full with ice. You'll dance to the air-conditioned rhythms of Felix Iceberg and his Twelve Icicles, and then you'll escort Miss Maxwell home and discuss Antarctica over a nightcap.

It sounded delightful.

I wish I worked for an advertising agency, Hawes thought. I'd leave the office at 5:00, and by this time, I'd be immersed in a tub of marti—

Time.

He looked at his watch.

Good God, what the hell was taking her so long? Impatiently, he reached for the buzzer again. He was about to press it when the door opened.

Felicia Pannet was easily the coolest-looking person he had seen all day. All week. All year. There was no other word for her. She was cool. She was, as a few junkies he knew might put it, "The coolest, man."

She had straight black hair clipped in what he supposed the coiffure con men called a Spider Cut or a Bedbug Cut or some sort of an insect cut. Whatever they called it, it was extremely short except for the tendrils, which, insect-like, swept over her forehead.

Her eyes were blue. They were not a warm blue. They were the blue you sometimes find on a very fair-skinned blonde or an Irish redhead. But fair hair softens the harshness of the blue in those cases; Felicia Pannet's hair had been poured from an ink-well, and it dropped the temperature of the blue eyes to some-where far below zero.

Her nose, like her hair, had been bobbed. The job was an excellent one, but Hawes could spot a nose bob at a hundred paces. Felicia's nose was a properly American, properly supper club, properly martini-glass-in-hand-spouting-latest-best-seller-talk nose. A cool nose for a cool woman. And her mouth, without lipstick, was thin and bloodless. For a moment, Hawes thought of Charles Addams. The moment passed.

"I'm sorry I kept you waiting," Felicia said. Her voice expressed no regret whatsoever.

"That's quite all right," Hawes said. "May I come in?"

"Please."

She did not ask for identification. He followed her into the apartment. She was wearing an ice-blue sweater and a black skirt. The thongs of pale-blue sandals passed through the spaces alongside her big toes. Her toenails were painted a bright red, as were her long, carefully manicured fingernails.

The apartment was as cool as the woman. Hawes was not an expert on modern furniture, but he knew the stuff in this apartment had not been purchased on Crichton Avenue. This was nine-months-wait, special-order furniture. It had the look and the feel of luxury.

Felicia sat.

"What's your name?" she said.

Her voice had the peculiarly aloof nasal twang Hawes had always identified with Harvard men. He had always assumed that the speech instructor at Harvard was a man who spoke through his nose and, emulated by his students, produced a generation of young men whose voices emerged through their nostrils rather than their mouths. He was surprised to hear the affected speech pattern and tone in a woman. He was half tempted to ask her if she was a Harvard graduate.

"My name's Hawes," he said. "Detective Hawes."

"Do I call you Detective Hawes or Mr. Hawes? Which?"

"Whichever you like. Just don't—"

"Just don't call me late for dinner," she completed unsmilingly.

"I was going to say," Hawes said flatly, annoyed that she thought he'd been about to use the old saw, "just don't waste any more of my time."

The rebuff produced nothing more on the face of Felicia Pannet than a slight lifting of her left eyebrow. "I had no idea your time was so valuable," she said. "What do you want here?"

"I've just come from the Jo-George Diner," Hawes said. "Do you know George?"

"I've met him, yes."

"He told me that you're his partner's girlfriend. Is that right?"

"Are you referring to Jo?"

"Yes."

"I suppose you might say I'm his girlfriend."

"Do you know where I can locate him, Miss Pannet?"

"Yes. He's out of town."

"Where?"

"He went upstate to do some fishing."

"When did he leave?"

"Early this morning."

"What time this morning?"

"About one o'clock."

"You mean this *afternoon*, then, don't you?"

"No, I mean this morning. I rarely say anything I don't mean, Detective Hawes. I mean this morning. One o'clock this morning. He worked late at the diner last night. He stopped by here to have a nightcap, and then he left for upstate. It must have been about one o'clock." She paused. Emphatically, she added, "In the *morning*."

"I see. Where did he go upstate?"

"I don't know. He didn't say."

"When will he be back?"

"Either late tonight or early tomorrow morning. He's due back at the diner tomorrow."

"Will he call you when he gets back?"

"He said he would."

"Are you engaged to him, Miss Pannet?"

"In a sense, yes."

"What does that mean?"

"It means I don't date any other men. But I haven't got his ring. I don't want it yet."

"Why not?"

"I'm not ready to marry him yet."

"Why not?"

"When I get married, I want to stop working. But I want to live the way I live now. Jo makes a decent amount of money. The diner's a going business, and he splits everything fifty-fifty with George. But he still doesn't make as much money as I do."

"Where do you work, Miss Pannet?"

"For a television packaging outfit. Trio Productions. Have you heard of it?"

"No."

Felicia Pannet shrugged. "Three people," she said. "A writer, a director, and a producer. They banded together and formed their own producing company. We package shows for a good deal of the industry. The *Pennsylvania Coal Hour* is one of our shows. Surely, you've seen that."

"I don't own a television set," Hawes said.

"Don't you believe in art?" she asked. "Or can't you afford one?"

Hawes let the remark pass. "And what do you do with Trio Productions?" he asked.

"I'm one of the original three, one of the trio. I'm the producer."

"I see. And this pays well, does it?"

"It pays extremely well."

"And Jo's cut of the business doesn't pay as well?"

"No."

"And you're not going to marry him until you can stay home and knit booties and raise a family on his earnings, is that—"

"Until I can live the way I'm living now, yes," Felicia said.

"I see." Hawes took the folded picture from his pocket. Slowly, he unfolded it and handed it to Felicia. "Ever see this man before?" he asked.

Felicia took the picture. "Is this your subtle way of getting my fingerprints?" she asked.

"Huh?"

"By handing me this picture?"

"Oh." Hawes smiled, beginning to dislike Miss Pannet intensely now, beginning to dislike Trio Productions, and beginning to dislike the *Pennsylvania Coal Hour* even though he had never seen the damned show. "No. I'm not trying to get your fingerprints. Would I have reason to want them?"

"How would I know?" she said. "I still don't know why you're here."

"I'm here to identify this man," Hawes said. "Do you know him?"

She looked at the picture. "No," she said. She handed it back to Hawes.

"Never saw him before?"

"Never."

"Possibly with Jo? Would he be one of Jo's friends?"

"All of Jo's friends are my friends. I never saw him with that man. Unless it's a bad likeness."

"It's a pretty good likeness," Hawes said. He folded the picture and put it in his pocket. His last chance seemed to have evaporated. If Jo Cort was on a fishing trip, there was no way to reach him before 8:00 tonight. There was no way to show him the picture. There was no way to identify the potential killer. Hawes sighed. "A fishing trip," he said disgustedly.

"He likes fishing."

"What else does he like?"

For the first time since he'd been in the apartment, Hawes saw Felicia smile. "Me," she said.

"Mmm," Hawes answered, refusing to comment on the taste that makes horse races and ball games. "Where'd you meet him?" he asked.

"He picked me up," she said.

"Where?"

"On the street. Does that shock you?"

"Not particularly."

"Well, that's the way it happened. Are you familiar with The Quarter?"

"Downtown? Yes."

"I was walking there one Wednesday. Our big show is Tuesday night, the *Coal Hour*. It's our only live show. We sort of relax right after it, generally take Wednesdays off unless there's a crisis in the office. I went down there that Wednesday to buy some jewelry. They have these unusual jewelry shops down there, as you may know."

"Yes," Hawes said. He looked at his watch. Why was he wasting time here? Why didn't he get back to the squadroom, where the company was congenial and pleasant?

"I was looking in one of the shop windows at a beautiful gold bracelet when I heard a voice behind me. It said, 'Would you like me to buy that for you?' I turned. A rather pleasant-looking man with a mustache and chin whiskers was standing behind me."

"Jo Cort?" Hawes asked.

"Yes. At first, I thought he was a Quarter artist. Because of the mustache and beard, you know. I said to him, 'Can you afford it?' He went into the shop and bought it for me. It cost three hundred dollars. That was the beginning of our relationship."

It figured, Hawes thought, and he began to form his own impressions of Jo Cort, a bearded jerk who'd spend three hundred dollars to pick up a girl like Felicia Pannet.

"He always wear this beard?" he asked, thinking of bearded men he had known in the past. One had grown the chin brush to hide the lack of a jaw. Another—

"Always," Felicia said. "He grew it when he was eighteen, and he's kept it ever since. I imagine he grew it because he was 4-F. A punctured eardrum. The beard made him feel more manly, I supposed. At a time when all of his friends were pretending to be men because of their uniforms. It's really quite attractive." She paused. "Have you ever been kissed by a man with a beard?"

"No," Hawes said. "I prefer my men with long sideburns instead." He rose. "Well, thanks a lot, Miss Pannet," he said.

"Is there anything you want me to tell Jo when I see him again?"

"By the time you see him again," Hawes said, "it'll be all over."

"*What* will be all over?"

"It," he said. "You might tell him that he picked an inconvenient time to go fishing. He might have been able to help us."

"I'm sorry," Felicia said, and again her voice indicated no regret.

"Yeah, well, don't lose any sleep over it."

"I shan't."

"I didn't think you would."

"May I ask a personal question?" Felicia said.

"Sure. Go ahead."

"That white streak in your hair. Where did you get it?"

"Why do you want to know?"

"I'm attracted by oddities."

"Like Jo Cort's beard and mustache?"

"I'll admit his beard attracted me."

"That and the three-hundred-dollar bracelet," Hawes said.

"It was a very unusual approach," Felicia said. "I don't usually allow myself to be picked up on the street." She paused. "You still haven't answered me."

"I got stabbed once," Hawes said. "They shaved the hair to get at the wound. When it grew back, it was white."

"I wonder why," she said, expressing real interest.

"It probably turned white from fright," Hawes said. "I've got to be going."

"If you ever want television work..." she started.

"Yes?"

"You'd make a good menace. In a spy story. The streak in your hair is loaded with intrigue."

"Thanks," Hawes said. At the door, he paused. "I hope you, and Mr. Cort, and the beard are very happy together."

"I'm sure we will be," Felicia Pannet said.

From the way she said it, he didn't doubt a word of it.

It was 7:35 P.M.

In twenty-five minutes The Lady would become a target. In twenty-five minutes the threat would become a reality, a potential killer would become a real killer.

It was 7:36 P.M.

In twenty-four minutes a Luger would spit bullets into the night. A woman would fall. A phone would ring, and the desk sergeant would say, "87th Precinct," and the call would be transferred upstairs, and Homicide North and Homicide South and police headquarters and lab technicians and assistant medical examiners would be called in to deal with a fresh homicide.

It was 7:37 P.M.

A pall of gloom had settled over the squadroom. Bert Kling was anxious to get home. He'd had a trying day at the waterfront, but he waited now with his leather jacket slung over his arm, waited for something to break, waited for Byrnes to pop out of his office and shout, "Bert! I need you!"

It was 7:38 P.M.

They sat around the desk looking at the letter again, Meyer, Carella, and Hawes. Meyer was sucking cough drops. His throat was worse, and he blamed it on the heat.

I WILL KILL THE LADY TONIGHT AT 8.

WHAT CAN YOU DO ABOUT IT?

The answer was in each of the detectives' minds.

NOTHING.

We can do nothing about it.

"Maybe it *is* a dog," Meyer said, sucking on his cough drop. "Maybe it's a dog called Lady."

"And maybe it isn't," Hawes said.

"Or maybe it's that hooker," Carella said. "Marcia. The Lady. If it's her, we're okay. She's covered, isn't she?"

"She's covered," Hawes said.

"Lady Astor, too?"

"She's covered," Hawes said again.

"Pete didn't send anybody to the ballet, did he?"

"No," Hawes said. "Bannister's clean. He didn't look anything like that damn picture."

"And nobody at the diner could identify it, huh?" Meyer asked. He swallowed and reached for another cough drop.

"I only saw one of the partners," Hawes said. "The other one's out of town." He paused. "The first one had the right idea, all right."

"Anybody want one of these?" Meyer asked, extending the box.

The other man ignored him. "What idea was that?" Carella asked.

"He was heading for a beer as soon as the eating crowd thinned. A place right down the street, he said. That's for me, too. As soon as I get out of here. You fellows join me? I'm buying."

"Where's the diner?" Carella asked, interested.

"Huh?"

"The diner."

"Oh. Thirteenth and The Stem."

"Near that bar, isn't it?"

"What bar?"

"The Pub. The bar where Samalson might have lost the glasses. The Pub. That was on North Thirteenth and Amberly."

"You think there's a connection?" Hawes asked.

"Well," Carella said, "if the guy ate at the Jo-George Diner, maybe he stopped for a drink at The Pub down the street. Maybe that's where he found Samalson's binoculars."

"Where does that lead us?"

"No place," Carella admitted. "But maybe it rounds out the picture." He shrugged. "I'm just batting it around."

"Yeah," Hawes said.

It was 7:40 P.M.

"This guy at the diner couldn't identify it, though, huh? The picture?" Meyer asked.

"No. It was a bum lead. All George wanted to talk about was how much he loved his partner, Jo. A son to him, that kind of kick. George is an orphan, all alone in the world. He's attached himself to this kid."

"Kid?" Carella asked.

"Well, he's thirty-four. But that's a kid to George. George is fifty-six."

"Funny partnership," Carella said.

"They met a long time ago."

"The usual partnership setup?"

"What do you mean?"

"In case of death, where there are no relatives, the surviving partner gets the business."

"I suppose so," Hawes said. "Yes. George mentioned that it was the usual partnership setup."

"Then if George kicks off, his partner inherits the diner, right? You said George was all alone in the world, didn't you? No relatives to make claims?"

"That's right," Hawes said. "What are you thinking?"

"Maybe Jo is getting itchy for George to drop dead. Maybe he's going to help him along tonight at eight."

Mention of the time caused each of the men to look up at the clock. It was 7:42 P.M.

"Well, that's a nice theory, Steve," Hawes said. "Except for a couple of items."

"Like?"

"Like...Does *George* sound like a *lady*?"

"Mmm," Carella said.

"And most important, we showed that picture to both George and the girlfriend of Cort. Neither of them recognized it. Our killer ain't Jo Cort."

"What made you think George was a lady, Steve?" Meyer asked. "The heat getting you?"

"Is he a queer or something?" Carella asked, refusing to drop it. "This George character?"

"Nope. I'd recognize it, Steve. He was legit."

"I was thinking...you know...some tie-in with The Lady." He tapped the letter. "But if he's not...well..." He shrugged.

"No, no," Hawes said, "you're on the wrong track."

"Yeah, you're right," Carella said. "I just thought...Well, the motive looked damn good."

"It's too bad it doesn't fit with the other facts," Meyer said, smiling. "Maybe we can change them to fit your theory, huh, Steve?"

Carella grinned. "I'm getting weak. This has been a busy day."

"You coming for a beer?" Hawes asked. "When this is all over?"

"Maybe."

"He had the right idea, George did," Hawes said. "As soon as his place cleared out, he was heading for *this*." Unconsciously, his finger tapped the Ballantine sign that had been used to form the figure eight in the letter. And then his finger stopped.

"Hey!" he said.

"The eight," Carella said.

"You think…?"

"I don't know."

"But…"

"Is the killer telling us? Is he telling us *where*?"

"A bar? At eight? Is that it?"

"Holy Jesus, Cotton, do you think so?"

"I don't know. Steve…"

"Hold it, Cotton. Now hold it."

The men were sitting on the edge of their chairs. The clock on the wall read 7:44 P.M.

"If it's a bar…Could it be The Pub?"

"It could. But who?"

"The Lady. It said The Lady. But if this damn eight had a hidden meaning…The Lady. The Lady. Who?"

The men were silent for a moment. Meyer took another cough drop and threw the box onto the desk.

"George may be headed for The Pub," Carella said. "He said a bar down the street, didn't he? And that's where Samalson lost the glasses. Maybe George *is* the victim. Cotton, I can't see it any other way."

"The Lady? How the hell can George Laddona be The Lady?"

"I don't know. But I think we—"

"Holy…!"

"What?" Carella stood up. "What?"

"Oh, Jesus. Translate it! You're Italian, Steve. Translate Laddona. The Lady! The Lady!"

"*La donna!*" Carella said. "Oh, my aching…Then he wants to be stopped. Goddammit, Cotton, the killer *wants* to be stopped! He's told us who and where. The killer—"

"But who's the killer?" Hawes asked, rising. And then his eye fell on the cough drop box on the desk, and he shouted, "Smith! Smith!"

And then they ran like hell out of the squadroom because the clock on the wall read 7:47 P.M.

Standing on top of the garbage can in the alley alongside The Pub, the man could see into the small window directly to the table where George Laddona was sitting.

He had not been wrong, then. He had known George's habits well enough to realize that he would stop at The Pub again tonight on the way home from the diner, would sit at his regular table, and would order a large schooner of beer. And when that was consumed, he would order another…Except that tonight he would not order another, he would never order another glass of beer again because at 8:00 he would die.

The man looked at the luminous dial of his watch. It was 7:52. In eight minutes, George Laddona would die.

He felt a sudden sadness. It was a thing he had to do, of course. It was the only way he could see. And he had planned it very well, had planned it so that he would be in the clear, so that even if he was suspected of motive, the facts would never tie in with him, the facts would never tie in with the man who'd be seen running down the street after the shooting.

And then to his own apartment. And then, tomorrow morning, back to work, unchanged, seemingly the same. Except that he would have committed a murder.

Would they stop him?

Had his letter been too subtle? Well, of course, he could not *tell* them. Could he have come right out and *told* them? But hadn't there been enough hints, hadn't he cleverly indicated what was going to happen, and shouldn't they have figured it out?

They had certainly figured out the rest. They hadn't been laggard about that, by God. He thought of the apartment he'd rented on Twelfth Street, the sleazy dump where he'd planned to spend the night, a place within walking distance of the shooting. He could no longer do that. They had found the apartment, had almost captured him. He could still remember shooting it out with the redheaded cop. That had been exciting, exhilarating. But now he couldn't use the apartment; he'd have to return to his own apartment. Was that wise? Suppose someone saw him? Should he simply wander the streets tonight? Should he put on the—

He stopped his thoughts abruptly and looked at his watch again.

7:55.

He reached into his pocket, felt something soft and warm, was surprised for an instant, and then remembered. And then his hand closed on something cold and hard, and he pulled it from his pocket, and the dim moon in the already dark sky illuminated the Luger with a deadly glitter.

He checked the magazine. It was a full clip.

Those magazines he had left in the apartment. Could they be traced? It didn't matter. He didn't have a license for the gun.

Would they trace it to the man from whom he'd bought it? No, that was unlikely. He'd bought it in the neighborhood, and he was sure it was a stolen gun. The man he'd bought it from had had all sorts of things to sell. This was some neighborhood, all right, some neighborhood, and still it had been good to him. It would be even better to him. After tonight it would be better.

He clicked off the safety.

It was 7:57.

He rested the Luger on the windowsill and carefully took aim at the back of George Ladonna's head. On his left wrist, the second hand of his wrist watch moved, and moved, and moved. The minute hand suddenly lurched. He saw it move, actually saw it move. It was 7:58. Would they stop him? He doubted it. The fools. The stupid fools.

Carefully, he kept his hand steady and waited.

At 8:00, just as he was going to fire, Cotton Hawes burst into the alley mouth.

"Hey!" he shouted. "You!"

The gun went off, but the killer's hand had yanked back an instant before he'd fired. Hawes lunged at him. The man turned, the Luger in his fist. Hawes leaped.

The gun went off again, and then the garbage can and the man rolled down clatteringly onto the alley floor. The gun was coming up again, turning to point at Hawes, a graceful weapon with a lethal discharge. Hawes swung. The gun went off wide. He swung again. He felt his fist collide with the man's face, and again he struck. And now the day's punishment, the heat, and the chase, and the seeming futility of the senseless desperation welled up in Hawes, exploded into his fists so that he battered the man until he was senseless.

And then, sighing heavily, he dragged him out of the alley mouth.

Inside The Pub, George Laddona was still trembling. The bullet had whacked into the tabletop, missing his head by perhaps two inches. He sat with a puzzled expression on his face, and his hands shook, and his lips shook as Hawes tried to explain.

"It was your partner," he said. "Jo Cort. It was your partner who shot at you, Mr. Laddona."

"I don't believe it," George said. "I just don't believe it. Not Jo. Jo wouldn't try to kill me."

"He would if he had a money-hungry girlfriend," Hawes said.

"You mean…you mean *she* was behind this?"

"Not actually," Hawes said. "At least, I don't think so. She didn't *tell* him to kill you, if that's what you mean. Felicia Pannet isn't the kind of girl who'd spend the rest of her life with a murderer. But she let him know what she wanted, and this probably seemed to him the only way he could get it for her."

"No," George said. "Not Jo," and he seemed ready to weep.

"Remember that picture I showed you today?" Hawes asked.

"Yes! That wasn't Jo! That was someone else. That's the man—"

"Wasn't it?" Hawes asked. He took the picture and a pencil from his pocket and hastily went to work on it. "Wasn't it Jo Cort?" he asked George, and he showed him the changed picture:

"Yes," George said. "Yes, that's Jo."

"Believe me," Hawes said. "He tried to kill you."

George brushed at his eyes. "He succeeded," he said.

In the police sedan, with the prisoner between Meyer and Carella on the backseat, Hawes drove leisurely back toward the precinct.

"Why'd you shout 'Smith!' when we were leaving?" Carella asked.

"Because I was looking at Meyer's damn box of cough drops, and all of a sudden I remembered."

"What'd you remember?"

"I remembered a landlady saying, *That's the way he looked this morning.* It didn't make sense at the time, but actually it meant he looked different this morning than he had looked on other mornings. And then this girl who lived across the hall from him. She said he'd reminded her of a *Russian spy.* All he needed was a bomb. And she thought it was funny that his name was Smith. When I asked her why, she said, *'Well, the cough drops and all, you know.'* I thought she was nuts at the time. But tonight, when I saw Meyer's box of Smith Brothers Cough Drops, it all clicked into place. Cort had shaved in the apartment the night before. That's what the scissors and straight razor were doing in that medicine cabinet."

"It figures," Carella said. "He's had that beard since he was eighteen. He thought he wouldn't be recognized without it."

"And he wasn't," Hawes said. He stopped for a traffic light. "But what I don't understand is how he planned to go back to the diner tomorrow morning? He'd be identified immediately."

"Maybe this'll help you," Carella said. "I found it in his pocket."

He flipped a soft, furry object onto the front seat. Hawes picked it up. "A false mustache and beard!" he said. "I'll be a son of a bitch!"

"I guess he planned to wear that until the real McCoy grew back," Carella said.

"He can grow a real long beard where he's going," Meyer said. "Anybody want a cough drop?"

Carella and Hawes burst out laughing.

"Man, I'm weary," Carella said.

"I guess O'Brien gets to see his ball game, huh?"

The traffic light changed. On the backseat Cort stirred into consciousness. He blinked and then mumbled, "You stopped me, didn't you?"

"Yeah," Carella said. "We stopped you."

"You've got the light, Cotton," Meyer said. "Let's go."

"What's the hurry?" Hawes asked. "We've got all the time in the world."

ABOUT THE AUTHOR

Photograph © Dragica Hunter

Ed Mcbain was one of the many pen names of the successful and prolific crime fiction author Evan Hunter (1926–2005). Born Salvatore Lambino in New York, McBain served aboard a destroyer in the US Navy during World War II and then earned a degree from Hunter College in English and psychology. After a short stint teaching in a high school, McBain went to work for a literary agency in New York, working with authors such as Arthur C. Clarke and P.G. Wodehouse, all the while working on his own writing on nights and weekends. He had his first breakthrough in 1954 with the novel *The Blackboard Jungle*, which was published under his newly legal name Evan Hunter and based on his time teaching in the Bronx.

Perhaps his most popular work, the 87th Precinct series (released mainly under the name Ed McBain) is one of the longest running crime series ever published, debuting in 1956 with *Cop Hater* and featuring over fifty novels. The series is set in a fictional locale called Isola and features a wide cast of detectives including the prevalent Detective Steve Carella.

McBain was also known as a screenwriter. Most famously he adapted a short story from Daphne Du Maurier into the screenplay for Alfred Hitchcock's *The Birds* (1963). In addition to writing for the silver screen, he wrote for many television series, including *Columbo* and the NBC series *87th Precinct* (1961–1962), based on his popular novels.

McBain was awarded the Grand Master Award for lifetime achievement in 1986 by the Mystery Writers of America and was the first American to receive the Cartier Diamond Dagger award from the Crime Writers Association of Great Britain. He passed away in 2005 in his home in Connecticut after a battle with larynx cancer.